THE IRRATIONAL DIARY OF
CLARA VALENTINE

THE IRRATIONAL DIARY OF CLARA VALENTINE

CORALIE COLMEZ

Coco Publishing

Paperback: 978-1-3999-2221-0
Ebook: 978-1-3999-2222-7

First printing, 2022

Coco Publishing

To all the girls who love maths

CONTENTS

How It Started

Ok, here I go – I'm starting a diary. Because something totally amazing happened today and I can't tell anyone. I can't even tell M! I. Can't. Tell M. Do you know when was the last time I didn't tell M something? Never, that's when!

She knows what's happened in my day a maximum of 75 seconds after *I* know about it. I notify her when I'm about to buy another 90s mesh top on Depop (so she can rein in my habit, but actually she always says I should do it), or when I've found a new show I like (so we can watch at the same time). I tell her what I'm having for dinner every day. I even text her my dreams in the morning, which is notably frowned on in most friendships but actually encouraged in ours. How can I keep something from her? I've already had to stop my fingers from phoning her without consulting me at least eight times. So for now, this is my solution – I'll write it all down in here and hopefully that'll be enough to keep me from blurting it out.

It's so strange to think that when I woke up this morning, I had no idea that this day would turn out to be anything other than normal – worse than normal, dreary, even. I woke up to my alarm ringing just as I was having a dream that I was getting *into* bed, so that set the tone for the day. I dragged myself to school feeling just about exactly as if I hadn't slept the whole night. I arrived with one minute to spare, only to be treated to the classic assembly speech about how we are the worst-behaved students the teachers have experienced in the entirety of their formidably long careers. Invigorating stuff.

I can't believe it's been only four weeks since the start of this school year. Everyone is already grey and haggard – you know, the February look. Except it's October. Summer holidays are but a distant memory, and they weren't even that great. Back in August, I was almost – almost! – excited for them to be over, and to be back in London with everyone. What was I thinking?

Well – I guess that what I was thinking was that this year would be like last year. I'd go to the park with M after school every day, and spend weekends watching movies featuring Leo back when he was still cute and trying out random alcohol combinations from the parental cupboards of whoever was hosting. I was forgetting that we're applying to uni this year. Our teachers seem to believe that this means we are no longer allowed the basic human right of time in the day to feed ourselves and sleep. Instead, we are to spend every minute doing homework and finding ever more creative ways to massage our most minute life experiences into impressive-sounding achievements for our personal statements.

I was in a medium-to-bad mood all day, getting progressively worse as the hours dragged on. My last period was Further

Maths. I sat next to Sayid, who was completely immune to the don't-talk-to-me vibes I was emitting and kept chatting happily about his mother's friend's cousin's wedding this weekend where there will apparently be an assortment of fit girls to meet.

When the bell rang I walked out quickly, rubbing my temples – the whole day had given me a headache. Outside was a light-less grey and drizzling mildly. The weather so closely represented my mood it was as if I had conjured it. All this to say that I was absolutely not prepared for the extraordinary thing that happened next.

I walked out of the door and in the corner of my eye I spotted Ty waiting to one side, looking all kinds of shades of gorgeous, his hair getting adorably curly in the rain. He was wearing all black – faded carpenter jeans, a soft T-shirt and a denim jacket. Unconsciously, I put my hands up to my own hair and confirmed what I already knew – rather than adorable curls, I was developing horrific frizz.

I gave Ty a tiny wave, wondering what he was doing there. And then – like we were in a film – he started walking towards me, so slowly and deliberately that it felt like the world was playing at half-speed. I was fixed to my spot, wondering if I was making a fool of myself and imagining things and he would turn out to be greeting someone behind me, but he walked right up to me, super close, close enough that when he talked in a low near-whisper I could hear every word as clear as the raindrops around us.

He opened his lips and they said, 'Clara, I need your help.'

| 1 |

Number of Pairs in a Set

Thursday 6th October – starting again

Wait, let's rewind a bit. I think we need some context – you know, for when people are looking over these to publish them after my death because I've become super famous and important. We can't have anyone wondering, *Who is M? Who is Ty? What is a personal statement?* (Because by then statements won't be a thing anymore as unis will have realised they are pointless. Can you tell mine is going great?)

So let's go back to this morning. On Thursdays, I start with Physics. That's followed by two hours of Maths with Mr Howard. Mr Howard is one of those teachers who I won't feel horrified at bumping into in the street a few years from now. He's young – Dad says, 'Who's the child teaching you?' He makes jokes. Occasionally they are funny. The best thing about Maths is that Mr Howard doesn't make a seating plan, which means M and I can sit next to each other in our favourite seats, all the way at the back of the class.

I slumped down in my seat, in the aforementioned bad mood, and M did the same.

M: Bad morning?

Me: Not great. You?

M: … [a groan]

Me: What happened?

M: News depression.

Me: Ah. Is it the story about how more young people are unemployed than ever before?

M: It's the whale with the plastic bags in its stomach. But thanks, now I can be depressed about unemployment too.

Me: Sorry. I saw the whale news, it's so sad.

M: I read it this morning, as I was staring at the plastic bag that I used *just last night* to carry Maltesers and grapes home. I'm a monster.

Me: You're not a monster.

M: I am though. Why did I get a plastic bag? I didn't need one! I could have carried everything in my hands! I am personally responsible for that story.

Me: You haven't used straws for years though. So you've saved lots of turtles.

M: Whatever. I killed a whale.

Me: You got us reusable coffee cups too, so that's even more saved turtles. We're probably reaching a whale-sized amount of turtles by now.

M: Ok...

Me: Ok?

M: Yeah.

Me: You need more? Umm... let's do another park clean-up! Remember last time they said a species of bird had just been spotted that they hadn't seen for 63 years.

M: [sitting up a bit, looking perkier] Yes—

Mr Howard: Girls, sorry to interrupt what looks like a fascinating conversation, but do you mind telling me what we're talking about up here?

M: Umm...

Me: We're talking about surds.

Mr Howard: Ok Clara, and what is a surd?

M: Umm...

Me: It's a root that you can't simplify.

Mr Howard: So how about you come up here and put these in their simplest form?

I walked up to the board.

Me: $\sqrt{49}$. This one is simple. 49 is a perfect square, it's the square of 7, so the square root of 49 is just 7, $\sqrt{49} = 7$.

Mr Howard: ...

Me: $\sqrt{45}$. Here, I can factorise 45 inside the square root as 9x5, and then we can split this up into two multiplied square roots: $\sqrt{(9x5)} = \sqrt{9}x\sqrt{5}$. 9 is a perfect square and 5 can't be simplified any further, so we get to $\sqrt{(9x5)} = \sqrt{9}x\sqrt{5} = 3\sqrt{5}$.

Mr Howard: ...

Me: $\sqrt{(20+12)}$. Here, you can't split up a square root with an addition, only with multiplication, so I need to do the adding first: $\sqrt{(20+12)} = \sqrt{32}$. Then I go through the same steps of factorising 32 and splitting up the multiplication, which gets me to: $\sqrt{32} = \sqrt{(16\times2)} = \sqrt{16}\times\sqrt{2} = 4\sqrt{2}$.

Mr Howard: [after a big sigh, gesturing for me to sit down] That was all very good – thanks, Clara. I expect you all to know the rules for simplifying surds like the back of your hands, because we will be using them all the time when we get to the next chapter [then he gave me one of those special teacher looks that mean bad things and good things at the same time].

M: How did you do that? I haven't heard a word he said since "good morning".

Me: I just, you know... listened.

M: Oh, that. Obviously I'm not going to do that.

Me: Well, do you want to hang out after school? I'll tell you about surds if you feed me crisps.

M: I can't believe I have to turn down such an exhilarating proposition, but I'm helping Mum at the youth centre.

Me: How did she get you to say yes to that?!

M: She was super sneaky. She totally took advantage of what I thought was a heart-warming mother-daughter conversation. I was complaining about the lack of interesting boys around and Mum said, "Miracle, connections happen when you're just living your life, not desperately searching for them."

(Side note: M has the kind of relationship with her mum where they talk about this type of thing, it's totally mind-blowing. Oh and yes, her full name is Miracle, which is why everyone calls her M.)

M: I said that was easy for her to say given that she has a lot of *connections* already. Then she said "What you need to do is put out into the world the energy that you want to get back, so if you do happy, interesting, fulfilling things, you'll attract that type of person."

Me: "Happy, interesting and fulfilling" does sound like a great boyfriend to me.

M: Well, I don't want a *boyfriend*. No offence.

(She said this pointedly, because, you see, I do have a boy-friend. He's called Sam and he's very sweet and thoughtful. He's cute too, pretty cute – like, indie-movie cute. Mum loves him. M thinks he's extraordinarily lame, but I get to have a nice time every weekend when he's in town, whereas she's always having to deal with guys whose idea of a conversation is describing their workout routine in detail, or who think Tarantino is god. Meanwhile she looks like Zendaya, so a lot of people like *her*. The list of her blocked people on Instagram is as long as a Dickens novel.)

Me: Yes, M, I'm not offended that you don't want a boyfriend. I am comfortable with my pedestrian life choices. Whatever, then, *a boy you're seeing*.

M: A lover.

Me: All right Madam Bovary. I thought you needed a husband to have a lover.

M: No – it's when you want a bit of romance with the sex, but not a full-on thing, you know. That's what I'm aiming for.

Me: But you haven't had the sex at all yet, so we are several steps removed from this.

M: [glaring at me] *Anyway*, after this invigorating bit of generational advice, which softened me up perfectly, Mum suddenly came up with a perfect example of an activity that would be happy, interesting and fulfilling: helping her run the party she's organising at the youth centre.

Me: Ah, clever. She really is a genius.

M: She did teach me everything I know.

Me: And that's saying something.

(No really – try not doing something M wants you to do and… well, you'll be doing the thing M wants you to do.)

After Maths we walked to lunch, only to see a big commotion around Alice. I will say that there has been a major improvement in my school life this year: now that our timetables are based on our interests and intellectual capacities, I am free from taking even a single class in common with Alice and Rayna. This has reduced our contact to mere brushes in the corridor here and there, which is perfectly survivable. Mum forced me to take Biology to AS Level last year in a deluded dream that I would one day follow in her footsteps at the hospital, thereby condemning me to one more year of sharing a class with them, but this year I am free. The bad thing about it is that I now only have Maths in common with M – otherwise, she takes Economics and Philosophy. It's been pretty hard to deal with, I'll be honest. But I guess the good thing about *that* is that I have noticed a marked reduction in how often teachers ask me to stop talking in class.

Seeing as I couldn't join the cluster of people around Alice clamouring for info – on the grounds of us hating each other – I had to listen in from a distance. All I could make out was something to do with Ty and his older brother.

'Do you think they're talking about why Ty hasn't been in school?' M whispered to me.

I shrugged, as if the thought hadn't crossed my mind, but the truth was, I *really* wanted to be part of that discussion. Because, you see, the biggest improvement in my life this year, even more than the aforementioned lack of Alice and Rayna, is the fact that Ty sits right in front of me in Maths. And that is good, because Ty is extremely hot. Like, HOT. He's also very nice and funny and all that. But when you're talking to him, to be honest, you're not thinking about that part. He's got a brooding resting face and a cute smile. He's got those muscles that do that ripple thing in the forearms. He's tall but not in the weird, unconscious-stoop-whenever-I-go-through-a-doorway way, more in the let-me-just-grab-that-for-you way. He has thick dark hair that he gets cut too short and then grows back too long and it looks like the softest thing in the world. And he has a really, really nice ass. The kind of ass that jeans were invented for. The kind that suddenly make you very creative about thinking up ways to engineer situations where you're walking up the stairs behind him. Dreaaaamy.

Unfortunately for me and for the state of the world, Ty is Alice's boyfriend. They've been together for a while – before Ty joined our school in sixth form. It seems impossible, on account of the fact that he is lovely and kind and she is the opposite of that, but there it is. Of course, there is also another fact, which is that Alice is stupidly beautiful. She looks like a Boden model

(I mean, she *is* a Boden model – I can't escape that fact because Mum gets all the catalogues and insists on going through them and circling stuff for me to look at even though I have never ever not once wanted anything from there) – healthy and sunny and perfect. I, on the other hand, am around chin-height for the average Boden model, and I have an unphotogenic nose. (M refuses to admit this but I have a bump if you look on my right side – that's why I've become an expert at making sure no photos of me from that angle ever make it onto social media.)

For the last couple of days, Ty hadn't been in class, and I had no idea why. He seemed totally fine last week. M tried to convince me to message him and ask what was going on, but I felt too embarrassed – I'd never texted him before. I did have his number in my phone, but that was just from one time last year where we ended up in a WhatsApp group together. Sure, we talk a bit in class, but to be honest, the stuff that comes out of my mouth in his presence is usually so bad that M has to kick me under the desk to shut me up. I can't help it! I get struck by the way his T-shirt fits a *little* bit snug on his shoulders and it just happens. M is fully supportive of my crush though, because she hopes it will mean an end to Sam. She herself doesn't share my Ty infatuation, seeing as she likes guys who look like they they've stepped out of French film about a vitamin D-deficient poet who's in love with his sister. If someone looks like they eat a balanced diet she is *not interested.*

I looked back over at the commotion. Rayna stood by Alice's side, lapping up the attention with her arm around Alice's shoulders, telling people off for talking over her.

Ugh, Rayna. We've been in the same school since we were six years old, like some cosmic joke played by our parents. I think they should study her to find out if there's a gene for bullying. What started off as giggling over my – I'll admit, late-ish – thumb-sucking phase in primary school grew into a lot worse at secondary. Once, she stole my pants from the swimming pool changing room after gym class. Then, she told everyone that I wasn't wearing any – and of course, I was in a skirt that day. It was the stuff recurring nightmares are made of. But eventually I had M on my side, and suddenly it was much easier not to care. And when I stopped caring, well, I guess that made it less fun for Rayna, so she stopped bothering me so much. The last few years she's been content with mostly ignoring me, which has been restful.

Alice and Rayna were friends from outside school, from when they were little – they met at Pony Club, because of course they did. When Alice joined our school, she slotted straight in with Rayna's crew, and now Rayna got to know more about Ty than I did.

So that's what had happened before I walked out of school at the end of the day and saw him there, Ty, waiting for someone. Waiting for... *me*.

'Clara, I need your help,' he said, and my heart skipped approximately thirty beats.

I stared at him in silence. In truth, I just forgot to answer because my heart had jumped all the way into my throat and my brain was occupied with thoughts such as, *Oh my god, oh my god,* and, *Is he possibly even* more *hot up close?*

He eventually gave up waiting for me to speak and went on: 'I'm looking for my brother. He's disappeared and... I have to find him.'

'Oh,' I said. Even that one sort-of-word was an effort. My mind was racing, but my mouth was working in slow-motion.

Ty spoke again, looking at the floor rather than me, as if he was arranging all his thoughts in his head as he was talking. 'Sorry,' he said. 'I want to say this in the right way, because my brother – Oli – he's... well, you need to understand what he's like.' He took a breath. 'Oli is sort of the *genius* of the family. Brilliant at maths, computing expert, taught himself to program totally on his own as a child. He didn't go to university. He didn't even bother doing his A Levels – my parents were livid with him. But he's been making money since he was super young anyway. He's one of those people that hack into companies' websites, but to help them increase their security. He was doing it already when he was fourteen – no one ever bothered asking how old he was because he was so good.'

'Wow...' I raised my eyebrows. I seemed to have recovered the power of speech, thankfully. 'He sounds pretty incredible. What's it like having a brother like that?'

'Well. Definitely both good and bad.' Ty gave a quick grin. 'He's the reason I'm taking Maths, you know. He always said to me that the stuff you learn in school is just to give you the ladder to climb up to a whole different maths world. And once you get there you can't believe how beautiful it is. He didn't seem to get that I can't even climb up the first rungs of the ladder.' He laughed dejectedly.

'Oh, right,' I said. I was so pleased Ty and I had a class in common that I'd never thought much about it. But it's true that he is pretty rubbish at maths – not like M, who can't be bothered to listen in class but will still manage the B she needs to get into Political Science at King's. Whenever Mr Howard calls on Ty in class, he mumbles random words that have nothing to do with the question. When we have tests, Ty spends most of the time looking out of the window. I think I've even seen him hand in a paper that he hadn't written a single word on.

'Anyway,' Ty said, 'a couple of days ago, Oli just – left. Suddenly. And I've had no news of him since. He left a note for me, here, look.' Ty handed me a folded-up piece of paper that was in his pocket. I could tell he'd been fingering it a lot.

*Ty - going somewhere for A bit. please don't
Tell Mum and dad i'm gone.*

*See you when i am back - and don't Worry i
am fine!*

oli

'It's a bit weird, right?' Ty said, looking worried, in a direct contravention of the note's instructions.

'It is,' I agreed. 'Is that definitely his handwriting?'

'Yes,' Ty shrugged.

'Is he left-handed?' I asked.

Ty's eyes opened wide. 'Yes! How did you know that?!'

I laughed. 'It's only because of the way the writing slants down. My dad is left-handed and his writing does that too. It didn't get passed on to me though – I'm right-handed.'

'Oh right.' Ty grinned. 'Well, you're clearly the right person to help me, already doing detective work.' His face got serious again. 'I mean, if you're up for helping me.'

'Of course I'll help you,' I said. 'Oli sounds amazing. I can't wait to meet him.' Not to mention the fact that there was no way I would say no with the way Ty was looking at me, all puppy-eyed.

Ty's face relaxed into a shiny smile. 'He *is* amazing,' he said. 'The most interesting person I know. He just... well, he has a very strong moral code, actually. It's just not always the same as the rest of society. Or the law.'

'But you haven't told me what I'm helping with exactly...' I pointed out.

'Oh yes, of course. So, when I first got Oli's note, I tried to find him. I went everywhere I could think of: the homes of a couple of friends of his that I know, his ex-girlfriend's place, the café he likes... No one had any idea where he was. So I took the key to Oli's flat from Mum's bag and I went over there. You could tell no one had been in for a few days – you could feel it in the air, that sort of cold smell. Otherwise, it looked exactly like always, a typical Oli mess with books in random places, clothes all over the floor and no food in the fridge.' Ty shook his head in mock disappointment. I could tell that he was really close to his brother even though they were obviously pretty different. The way his mouth curled up at the corners when he described how smart Oli was. It was... well, it was seriously cute.

'In his flat,' Ty went on, 'I found his second laptop. It's the one he uses if his main one is running a program that takes a few hours, or if he wants to go work in a café. He is very precious about his main laptop.' Ty laughed. 'He wouldn't let that one anywhere near strangers holding liquid. Anyway, when I saw the computer, I thought... well, I know the two laptops are linked in some way. Don't ask me how, but he set it up so that one of them updates when you do something on the other. So I figured that if I can get into the laptop, I'll be able to see what he's working on, or maybe even where he is.'

'Yeah, that could definitely work!' I exclaimed. This all sounded quite exciting, to be honest.

'The only problem is...' Ty went a bit red. 'I can't actually get into the laptop. Because Oli programmed it so that there isn't a password or anything; instead, you need to solve a maths question to get in.'

'He... what?'

'Yeah, he did it when he still lived at home – when this was his only computer. He said it was to keep me out of his business, but I think he actually sort of wished I would find the answers. It was like he was setting me a challenge – but of course I never did manage to get in. He's programmed it with hundreds of questions and every time you turn it on you get one at random. I've tried to turn the computer off and on a few times to see if eventually it comes up with a question I can do but...' He fell silent and looked sheepish.

'So you want me to help you with the maths question?'

'Yes,' he said. There was a very irresistible look of hope on his face. 'You seem to always know how to do the questions in class... I don't know how you do it. It's so funny when you get Mr Howard exasperated because you're the only one who knows the answer again.'

He smiled at me and I swallowed hard. He'd noticed that? This whole time I thought he barely realised who I was, but Ty had been walking around with thoughts and opinions about me just living in his head?

'There's no one else I could ask,' Ty went on, as if he hadn't just said something world-spinning. 'I know I'm grasping at straws, but this computer is the only idea I've had. I don't want to sit around waiting to find out what Oli is up to. I at least want to know what to expect before it happens!'

I followed Ty through narrow residential streets for about fifteen minutes until we got to his house. It was a small house, divided into two flats – his family lived in the top one. I'd always imagined his house to be of the Alice type: sprawling, garish, with a mysterious number of staff silently coming in and out of rooms (that's what I remember from the only time I've been in-vited to Alice's – a long-ago birthday party at the age when your parents make you invite the whole class.) In reality, it was a little place with a crooked staircase and a small balcony (the bottom flat had access to the garden). The walls were all white, with framed Bollywood posters from the '60s over the couch, and a handful of family photos above the out-of-use fireplace. One was a photo of what looked like Ty's parents on their wedding day, looking very young and happy, his mother in a short white dress and his father in tan trousers and a matching waistcoat. On either side of them were their parents, Ty's grandmothers in bright saris and his grandpas in long tunics and wide trousers. Everyone was smiling in the way that Ty does, with his mouth and his cheeks and his eyes, and even his whole body.

Ty told me that both his parents were academics – his father an astrophysicist and his mother a historian. The living room had books everywhere, on shelves all over the walls, with titles like *Ladies of (Mis)fortune – the role of prostitutes in Victorian England*, or *Neutrino Oscillations*. We didn't stay in there long, but I'm pretty sure I spotted his parents' names on some of the books.

The floor was wood, with an indigo woven rug in front of the sofa, and a burnt-orange one in the small hallway to the bedrooms. The flat was empty – it was still a few hours to dinner time, when I guessed Ty's parents would come home. I followed him as he led me towards his bedroom. On his door there was a little chipped sign that read *Tycho's room*. I was surprised – I'd always assumed Ty was short for Tyler.

'It's after Tycho Brahe,' he explained. 'My dad liked the name from when he first heard it at school; he thought it sounded mysterious. But honestly, I'm not sure why you would call your child after someone who died from a too-full bladder, even if they were a genius scientist. Oli has certainly found it relentlessly entertaining to make jokes about it, every single day since my birth.' He smiled to himself like he was remembering something. 'Mum named Oli – so then Dad got to name me. She says Oli is called that because he came three weeks early and she never had the time to finish what she was reading at the time: *Oliver Twist*. But Oli's never accepted that explanation, he maintains it's after the guy in *Lady Chatterley's Lover*.'

We entered his bedroom, and Ty got a grey laptop out from behind some books on his bookshelf. We sat on the bed with the laptop between us and I suddenly realised that shortly, I was going to have to solve an unknown maths question right in front of Ty. While sitting on his bed. What had I got myself into?

I started to feel extremely hot. There were beads of sweat on my upper lip and I wiped it, discreetly I hoped, with my arm. Now I wasn't sure whether I was more nervous about the maths question, or about looking like a mess.

I looked around to distract myself. Ty's room was small but bright with a big window looking out onto the little back garden, in which I could see an obese ginger cat prowling and destroying flowers. His room was pretty neat, with just the nice level of mess – the duvet bunched up, football clothes on the floor, books arranged every which way on the shelves. There was a small built-in closet, a stool with clothes thrown onto it, and the bed. There was no desk and I smiled to myself because I don't have a desk either, which I've been fighting about with Mum forever. (She says I need one to work properly but I just work on my bed anyway and I'd rather have more space. I eat on my bed too which is another rich seam of arguments.) I liked the thought of Ty doing homework on his bed like I did.

His walls were white and his curtains and sheets were a dark blue. There were posters blu-tacked to the wall – a couple of footballers (Mo Salah and another one I didn't know), some postcards and some photos. One was of him with Alice, but mostly they were arty film photos with lots of lens flare which I assumed he had taken with the old Olympus camera that was hanging from a hook on the wall. There was also a scratched-up teddy bear with a missing eye on one shelf, next to a couple of glowy toys like the ones you get in the gift shop section of a science museum.

I focused back on Ty, who opened up the computer to show me the words that popped up on the screen. I read them carefully:

Question 257: If there are 143 people in a room, and everyone shakes hands with everyone else, how many handshakes take place?

I turned the question round in my head. Ty was looking at me intently in a way that was very unnerving and made me feel certain that I had a huge spot forming on my cheek or something in my teeth. The intense look somehow made him seem even more beautiful, which didn't help me to relax.

'We can turn it off and on again, if you want to try a different question,' he suggested in a febrile voice.

'No, no,' I said. 'I... I really think I can do this one. I just need to think about it carefully. Can you give me some paper and a pen?'

Ty scrabbled around on his shelves and came back with a small notebook and a blue ballpoint pen. I started scribbling furiously.

I needed to make sure I was thinking carefully, not getting into a mess and double-counting myself. Starting with the first person is always the best way to get to understanding the pattern. So, I imagined that the people in the room were all numbered from 1 to 143 and thought about Ms Number 1.

No one had exchanged handshakes yet, so Ms Number 1 had to shake hands with everyone (apart from herself) – that meant shaking hands with Number 2 through to Number 143, which was 142 handshakes.

Then, Ms Number 2 had already shaken hands with Number 1 when it was Number 1's turn, and she couldn't shake hands with herself, so she had to shake hands with Numbers 3 through 143, which was 141 handshakes.

Then it was Ms Number 3's turn. She'd already shaken hands with Numbers 1 and 2 when it was their turn, and couldn't shake hands with herself, so she shook hands with Numbers 4 through to 143, which was 140 handshakes.

This was an easy pattern to simply repeat, each time decreasing the number of handshakes by one, until we reached Ms Number 143 who didn't have anyone's hands left to shake, since they'd all shaken hers when it was their turn.

Now I just needed to add up all those handshakes: 142 from Number 1, 141 from Number 2, 140 from Number 3, all the way until 2 from Number 141, 1 from Number 142, and 0 from Number 143.

In other words, I needed to do the sum: $1 + 2 + 3 + ... + 140 + 141 + 142$

I could have used a calculator, but actually, I knew how to do this one really quickly! It's one of my favourite formulas because of the story behind it. The famous German mathematician, Gauss, back when he was a child, was being a nightmare with his friends in class so much that his teacher got exasperated and gave them a problem to keep them quiet (a common maths-teacher tactic, I suppose). He told them to add up all the numbers from 1 to 1000 in silence, thinking that they'd sit there adding everything one by one and taking forever.

That was without counting on Gauss' genius – he thought for a second and realised that if you were looking for the sum:

$S = 1 + 2 + 3 + \dots + 998 + 999 + 1000$

You could also reverse the order and write it down as:

$S = 1000 + 999 + 998 + \dots + 3 + 2 + 1$

Then if you added those two equations column by column, you got:

$S = 1000 + 999 + 998 + \dots + 3 + 2 + 1$
$S = 1 + 2 + 3 + \dots + 998 + 999 + 1000$

$2S = 1001 + 1001 + 1001 + \dots + 1001 + 1001 + 1001$

– all the terms were equal to 1001!

The 1001s got added 1000 times (because there were 1000 terms in S to start with), which meant that in the end:

$2S = 1000 \times 1001$
So $S = 1000 \times 1001 / 2 = 500500$

And Gauss got it all done in record time, to his teacher's annoyance.

I used the same trick for our question: $142 \times 143 / 2$, and got a result of 10153 (which I calculated three times in my phone to make sure). I wrote the number down and turned to Ty with my heart pounding.

'I think I've got it...' I said slowly.

His face spread into the biggest and shiniest smile you've ever seen, and he turned the computer towards me.

'Wait,' I added, 'do you know what happens if I get it wrong?'

Ty shook his head. 'He never told me that.'

'Well, I guess those self-destruct things only exist in James Bond films.'

I tried to laugh but the sound came out strangled and thin. My heart was pounding hard as I typed in the numbers, double-checking obsessively that I hadn't made a typo. *Does self-destruction really only exist in movies?* I vaguely remembered reading an article about Russian spies who'd set fire to their hotel room because of a self-destructing briefcase. Or had I read that in a novel? In any case, they could poison someone by spraying his face, so self-destruction didn't seem very far-fetched...

I pressed enter and held my breath as the computer hummed. A black tick appeared on the screen and I nearly fainted with relief. Even better: Ty grabbed my arm in excitement, leaving what felt like a hot handprint. If I thought my heart had been beating hard before, well – it was just bouncing around in there now like a wrecking ball.

We watched together as the tick faded (Oli might be a maths and computer genius but his graphic design skills leave a lot to be desired. The check disappeared into darkness in a pixelated mess). Instead of the desktop screen we were expecting to see, though, another question came up.

'There's another one!' I said in a half-whisper, stating the obvious. 'Do you know how many there's going to be?'

Ty shook his head. 'I thought there would only be one,' he told me, looking distressed again.

I slowly read the words on the screen and my heart sank. It didn't seem like such a hard question, but I didn't have the first clue how to get started.

> **Question 349:** How many people do you need to have in a room to get at least a 50% chance that two of them share the same birthday?

My first thought was that there were 365 days in the year (if we forgot about leap years) so the answer would be half of that – around 183 people. But that seemed much too simple. And then I thought about our class – there were 31 of us, three with the same birthday and another pair on a different day! It seemed like a lot of coincidences if my guess of 183 people was correct.

I turned it round in my head for a bit but I couldn't think of anything else. 'Ty... I'm really sorry, but I just can't think of how to do this one,' I said, reluctantly. I felt really disappointed with myself. Honestly, after I'd got that first one right, I thought I could do anything!

Ty looked disappointed too, which I couldn't bear for more than one second. 'I could work on it more at home,' I heard my mouth say. 'I don't know if I'll get it, but...'

That perked him up a lot – his eyes lost some of their sad-puppy look. 'That would be amazing. Thank you so much, Clara!' He smiled. 'You were great with that first one. I would never, ever have got it. I'm sure you'll get this one too.'

What if I don't? a little voice inside my head piped up. Why was I promising to do something I didn't know if I could do? I mean, I know *why* – Ty grabbing my arm when he talked is why. But still, it was a pretty stupid thing to do.

He walked with me back to his front door and I promised I'd call him as soon as I got the answer. He gave me a quick good-bye hug and leaned in close into my ear. 'Please don't tell anyone about this,' he whispered. 'I don't want anyone to know, not until I know what Oli is up to.'

'I won't tell anyone,' I promised.

'Not even M.' It wasn't a question.

'Not even M,' I repeated, even though I could already feel the overwhelming need to talk to her.

I walked home in a sort of daze. As soon as I was on my own again, the past few hours with Ty felt like a crazy dream. I was involved in searching for his missing brother! There was a mysterious note! I wondered what Oli could be up to. Hackers could be involved in anything, really – influencing elections, stealing money, infiltrating the dark web… it was hard not to let my imagination run wild with possible scenarios.

I still felt high from having solved that first maths question. It had been such a thrill knowing that I could figure out the answer. I had almost *felt* it happening inside my head, as if my brain was a muscle lifting a heavy weight – all the parts working together to get to the solution. I actually couldn't wait to get home and settle in my room to think more about the second question and get that feeling in my head again, with everything slotting into place and all my thoughts in a perfectly straight line pointing towards the answer.

By the time I got home, the day's dismal grey has faded into black. It was no longer raining but the ground was soggy and rotting leaves carpeted every bit of the pavement. The air still held on to the dampness and everything I was wearing had slowly become soaking wet. I hung up my jacket gratefully in the entrance at home, changed into dry sweats and towelled my hair. I lay down on my bed, turning the new question round in my head.

Then my phone buzzed. It was a message from Sam: *I can't wait to see you tomorrow!* it said, with a bunch of multicoloured hearts. I fell back on my pillows.

Sam. If I'm honest, I hadn't thought about him all afternoon. I felt sick with myself. I'd been mindlessly touching the place on my arm that Ty had grabbed and daydreaming like an idiot, as if it meant anything... Ty had just asked me for a favour, as a friend, obviously. I mean – we'd spent the whole time under Alice's angel face in that photo! And here I was letting my stupid mind race around, when I have the loveliest boyfriend. I sent Sam lots of hearts back, swallowing down guilty feelings.

Sam has been my friend literally since the day I was born: we were born on the same day and his mum was in the hospital room with my mum. He graduated from just friend to boyfriend when we were thirteen and he got down on one knee with a jelly ring and declared that he was 'very much in love with me and would be delighted if we could be a couple.' I said yes because as far as I knew, no one else in my class had a boyfriend yet, which made it an extremely exciting event. Mum does say that when we were little she caught us playing "doctor" (she always does the air quote thing with her fingers when she says it). She giggles every time she mentions this, so I've never asked her for any details. All I remember is lots of sleepovers, inventing a secret language, and running in the garden together all summer long. I think Mum harbours the secret hope that we will get married, which is why we're allowed up in my room by ourselves and she makes sure to always knock before coming in.

I love Sam. I mean, I really love him. He's my best friend, in sort of the opposite way that M is my best friend. When it's just the two of us, we have a perfect time. But there's always been this thing where... I don't know how to explain it. I can't get him to fit in with the rest of my life. It's like he's this imaginary friend from my childhood and when other people are around he turns into a wooden puppet. I mean, when I take him to parties, for example, he just stays silently in a corner the whole time, unless I'm talking to him.

M and him transform into the worst version of themselves around each other. It's as if they are opposite magnets pushing each other away into two extremes of assholeishness. M becomes unable to sustain a conversation without it ending in a huge argument (even if she agrees totally with what Sam is saying). Meanwhile Sam morphs into one of those people desperate to be liked, with no individual thoughts or personality. And he develops a very irritating posh accent. So anyway, I stopped trying. It's only ever just me and him, like when we were kids.

Well – not exactly like when we were kids. See, we've got this tradition of making our shared birthday a BIG DAY every year. When we turned seven we spent all our pocket money on sweets and ate the whole lot in one go. When we turned fourteen we snuck into a Rated R movie (that was a bit traumatizing, actually). Next birthday, when we turn eighteen, is meant to be the BIG BIG DAY. As in, the day we have sex. (I can hear M's voice in my head now: *you mean the first time you have penis-in-vagina sex.* Yes M, that is what I mean).

Our birthday is in March, so around five months away now. I'm having major doubts. I'm just not sure I want my first time to be with him. I've always imagined that it would be, I don't know, something that you just feel you absolutely need to do *right that moment.* Only I haven't felt that with Sam. Ever. Otherwise, well, I'd probably forget about the birthday tradition pretty quickly... At the same time, I can't really imagine my first time being with anyone else. He's been *all* of my first times. How could I not want Sam to be this one too?

Anyway, in the meantime, we hang out on Fridays. Sam goes to Harrow (ugh) and he's a week boarder, so every weekend he comes back to the city and stays with his parents. Our Friday dates always end the same way thanks to Mum's aforementioned blessings on the relationship and the wide berth she gives my bedroom when Sam is round. I mean, yeah we haven't had sex yet, but we do other stuff. Mostly, Sam is the one who does the doing. Me, I just feel... confused. Even after some intense internet research I'm still unsure about whether I'm meant to do things slow or fast and squeeze hard or soft. And also, when they are circumcised, apparently you are supposed to use lube? It doesn't help that every time things start we both go completely silent, as if by not talking we can pretend that nothing is happening. I swear the silence in those moments is extra heavy and hard to break. So mostly I sort of do over-clothes rubbing, and apart from that I'm just waiting until March and we'll see what happens then.

Oh god, I got very side-tracked with the Sam stuff there. Reader from the future – please feel free to ignore and I'll have more mystery-solving for you soon!

| 2 |

The Birthday Problem

Friday 7th October

Well, I have to warn you that today's entry does not contain any mystery or mathematical breakthroughs, as I haven't had the time to work on Oli's question. Please accept my apologies, and we'll be back to our regular programming soon.

Sam has just left to go back to his after we hung out tonight. It's funny, I don't think about him very much during the week, and then on Friday evening, just before he arrives, I have this feeling that I miss him and can't wait to see him. And every time he gets here and it's just – I don't know. He's just the same old Sam.

He met me on the canal and we walked around for a bit. The weather was nice, surprisingly, and the light made everything look like a romantic movie. Sam likes holding hands with our fingers all criss-crossed which I find a bit irritating. Your hands get sweaty and you can't check your phone and stuff. But I held his hand anyway because he was being cute about it. His hair is pretty overgrown and curly at the moment. He hates it, he's always hoping some new hair gel will fix all his issues, or else cutting it super short. It never works – the hair just springs back to its natural state, no matter what he tries. I like it best like it is now, a bit long, when he has to shake the curls out of his eyes all the time.

We wandered around until it was time to eat. Mum let us take our food into my room so we ate on the floor and put *Charades* on without really watching it. It was still on when we started kissing.

Sam's a really good kisser. I mean, I don't have any other kissing to compare it with but it's objectively good. He does these soft kisses where your lips barely touch, just sort of skim each other, and you're breathing each other's breath. And then he'll switch straight into deep ones where you think you're going to melt into one person, and he'll lick my lips and bite them until they feel tingly.

When we started going out, four years ago, we used to just lie on the bed and kiss for hours and hours. Every time it felt like the most exciting, perfect thing you could ever do. Now the kissing lasts for five minutes before his hand starts creeping up slowly, over my hips and under my top. Slowly, slowly, up along my ribcage. Even though we do this every week, he always does it the same way, like a horse-tamer making steady movements with a wild young foal or something. As if by going slowly, I won't notice what his hand is doing until it's on my breast – *gotcha!* Except we do it every time, so... he knows I want it to happen. He knows it always happens. I don't understand why we're still doing the slowly, slowly thing.

I know that it's not his fault. Not *just* his fault, I mean. It's on me as well. It's because of the silent mode we both go into as soon as his hand starts doing its thing. Every time I think I'll say something or do something different, but in the end nothing comes out of my mouth. I always think – *it's just us. It's just Sam! You can say anything to Sam!* But the words don't come out.

Afterwards, we magically recovered the power of speech. We lay down next to each other, with my head resting on the little dip in his shoulder that feels like it was made especially for me. I could feel that he was dreading going home.

Sam isn't close to his parents. It's not in a way where he fights with them or they are awful or anything like that. He just... He told me once that he thinks they don't actually like him – I mean, like the person that he is. He was their golden baby, the child they had really late after thinking they could never have any – a perfect son. That lasted only until he learned to talk and dashed all their plans for him. They wish he was more ambitious, made friends with the right boys at school, was invited to over to theirs for Shabbat, talked their dads into giving him an internship, dated one of the girls from synagogue. Instead, Sam is sweet, not ambitious. He's a Shabbat-dinner-avoider. He's a B student. He's always making friends with the underdogs. He wants to be a primary school teacher. And the worst: I'm not Jewish.

I chattered away, trying to make him forget about the heavy Friday-evening feeling in his stomach. I asked about his friends, who I feel like I know quite well since I hear about them so much (when actually, I haven't met them more than once or twice). But I swear, read any book set in a boys' boarding school and you basically know all about these guys. It's a world of clichés: who's getting addicted to cocaine; who's having sex with a teacher; who thinks who tried to see him naked; who punched who; whose mum is an alcoholic; whose dad is on trial for fraud or sexual harassment. They're all very happy to live in the '50s over there.

Sam left a bit late. I mean, late enough that I know his parents will be mean about it. As he was hugging me goodbye, my phone beeped. It was a text from Ty: *Thank you for yesterday. I feel so much better about everything now that you're helping.*

Ugh, so many butterflies in my stomach. This whole thing would be easier if Ty refrained from making statements that any reasonable person would agree could be obsessed over and dissected.

'Everything ok?' Sam asked.

'Oh. Yes,' I said, slipping the phone back into my pocket.

'You just seemed like you were thinking about something else tonight.'

I felt bad. He was right, I'd been distracted. I'd actually been thinking about the birthday problem a lot – I couldn't stop myself. I hadn't had any time to really consider it properly and it was running around in my head. Plus, my brain was creating more and more improbable scenarios for what Oli might be up to, and if it continues, I'll soon convince myself that the Russian mafia is on my tail.

'I'm just nervous about uni stuff,' I said. 'I have less than ten days left.'

'Oh yeah. Cambridge, huh.'

'Don't say it,' I protested. 'You might jinx it.'

He made a gesture like he was zipping his lips together. 'Hey,' he said. 'Could you look at the application I'm sending next week? It's to work in a school over the summer. The deadline is next Friday.'

'Yes of course!' I exclaimed. I felt overly happy that I could do something to help him, like it would make up for the stuff I wasn't telling him about.

'Thanks.' He smiled.

'I don't know how useful I'll be,' I warned him.

He shrugged. 'I just trust your opinion. I'll send it to you tonight, ok?' He kissed me goodbye. Another very good kiss.

I still felt a bit weird when Sam left. I didn't realise it would be this hard to keep a secret. How do people do it? This whole day has been weird, really. Ty was back in school and when M saw him sitting in front of us she waved her hands about all excitedly and mouthed a silent scream at me. Meanwhile, Ty and I were studiously avoiding each other and pretending nothing happened yesterday. Well, Ty was doing that and I was acting like a malfunctioning robot. I could see myself from the outside being strange, but I was powerless to do anything about it. I just couldn't bring myself to look straight at M – I felt like the second she saw my eyes she would somehow know everything that I wasn't telling her. We had a weird, whispered conversation.

M: He's back!

Me: I can see that.

M: Ask him where he was!

Me: No!

M: Fine, then I'll ask him.

Me: No! that's embarrassing!

M: You're being weird.

Me: I'm not being weird! You're being weird, leave him alone!

Well. Obviously I *was* being weird. M squinted at me and then shrugged. I sighed with relief – I seemed to have got away with it. I quickly changed the subject.

Me: Hey, how was the thing at your mum's work?

M: It was great actually! The whole event was very sweet. Apparently it was World Pizza Day? That's what Mum claimed, anyway. It was a popular theme, though she didn't manage to convince anyone to go for the cashew cheese and cauliflower crust options. All the kids got to build their own pizzas.

Me: What was your role?

M: As you can imagine, thirty kids each building their own pizza created some logistical and cleanliness challenges. But I also got to assist with the creative process, both by suggesting flavour combinations and also by advising on pizza-topping layout. So it wasn't so bad.

Me: And you got to eat pizza.

M: And I got to eat enormous amounts of pizza.

Me: And did you feel happy and fulfilled like Amanda promised?

M: Well, I must have been setting off some happy and fulfilled vibes, because...

Me: Ooooh, because what?!

M: So, the first thing I noticed when I arrived was a beautiful guy who was also helping with the party. Camel-length eyelashes, major cheekbones... great outfit too: a faded T-shirt in the perfect shade of orange, black cords and trainers just the right amount of scuffed. Turns out he works at the centre a couple of days a week. He told me that he works there because his younger brother got killed by a stray bullet when they were kids. He says it feels like he has lots of little brothers and sisters when he's there.

Me: Oh my god. That's so sad.

M: Yeah. I mean, he wasn't saying it for sympathy or anything. It just came up in conversation. We talked the *whole* time. He was so interesting. And he's called Leo, which we can agree is a very hot name.

Me: It is. I do agree. So, what does he do the rest of the time? Is he studying?

M: No, he's a photographer.

Me: Wait, how old is he?

M: He's thirty-two.

Me: Thirty-two!

M: Age is just a number, Clara.

Me: Yeah, a number that tells you how old he is.

M: You don't even think about that when you're talking. We had so many things to say to each other.

Me: Ok...

M: We just talked, Clara. You can relax. It made the day fun, that's all.

She rolled her eyes at me, no longer looking pleased. I backed off, because I didn't want to add an argument on top of secret-keeping to my list of friendship transgressions. School is at least 67% less enjoyable when M is annoyed with me.

After class, when we were crossing the hall towards lunch, we saw Alice with her mother, talking to the headteacher. It's so interesting meeting people's parents. It's like finding that piece of the puzzle you've been looking all over for. Like, *of course, I understand now.* Not that everyone turns out at all like their parents, but you can normally see how the family dynamic happens. For example, M's mum, Amanda, is extremely awesome. She's also – let's call it… the opposite of boring. She and M have about 97% the same personality.

But then again, M could have turned out like Eloise, whose parents are some of the last true hippies standing. Their house is full-time yoga, chanting, meditation, crystals everywhere, marijuana plants in the bathroom. Eloise sits next to me in Physics and wears a suit every day – as in, a suit that she went to buy, on purpose, in a shop, that looks exactly like our uniform from before sixth form, with a tie and everything. She says she missed the uniform and didn't want to have to think about what to wear. So I guess that's another way it can go.

Unfortunately, you don't usually get to meet people's parents that often, unless you're friends enough with them to go to their house. Even then, lots of my friends don't like having people over and are a bit embarrassed by their parents. At least that's not the case with me. I mean, yes, Mum is one of those overly invested ones who ask all the questions at parent-teacher evenings, but I can rely on her to behave herself around my friends, for the most part. And she dresses pretty well. I even convinced her to branch out from her dark-wash J Brands and get a pair of those vintage Levi's that make your bum look like the peach emoji. And Dad has got the laid-back, I-trust-my-teenage-daughter-completely vibe down to a t, which my friends love. Also, well, let's just say that most of my female teachers, plus Mr Johnson, are suddenly extra sweet to me when he's in the building. It's a bit gross but I do enjoy the favourable treatment, as well as their not-so-subtle efforts to figure out if Dad is still single.

Anyway, Alice's mum seemed to be making a lot of fuss about something, and to be fair to Alice she had that sullen, *why must you embarrass me so?* look on her face and wasn't saying anything.

I swear, every time I see Alice's mum, there has been yet another major alteration to her facial features. This time, her eyebrows had been dyed a disturbingly dark shade of brown. She was wearing a very tight pair of gold jeans. I couldn't believe she was able to even walk in them. She didn't *look* like she was in pain but then again, she didn't look like she was experiencing any kind of emotion because her face was pretty much static. Sayid joined M and me, and he looked over with appreciation.

Sayid: Wow, she must have been so hot when she was our age.

M: Seeing as only about twenty percent of her has been left unaltered, you have no idea what she looked like when she was our age.

Sayid: Whatever. I'll take her, plastic and all.

M: That's rape culture right there!

Sayid: Oh shush. It's just an expression.

M: That's exactly the point! If this stuff is just an expression, then you see how rape culture keeps being propagated.

Sayid: Clara, please be on my side [he grinned at me.]

Me: Hmm, I think that Sayid was just being gross, not rape-culture-y.

Sayid: See? I'm a feminist, me.

Me: A gross feminist.

Sayid nodded, entirely happy with that assessment.

I watched Alice's mother kiss Principal Hartwood on both cheeks and make sparkly fake smiles at him. Oh, if only Alice's dad wasn't hoping to become Minister for Education in the near future. Then he'd have sent Alice to some fancy boarding school far, far away from here instead of making her slum it with the rest of us.

Anyway, the really interesting thing wasn't Alice's mum per se – it's what happened next. Out of the corner of my eye, I saw Ty walk in, clock them, and promptly turn around and disappear. I looked over at M but she hadn't noticed.

Well, it seems all *isn't* blissfully well in Ty and Alice's world, if he doesn't even want to bump into to her and her mum. Maybe Mr and Ms Perfect aren't so perfect after all. Though ugh – this is another thought I'm not supposed to be having!

Saturday 8th October

Finally, some maths! Unfortunately, in the form of mathematical disasters. I've spent most of the day so far working on Oli's question but, spoiler alert, I've got nowhere.

I woke up super early, before six, and couldn't go back to sleep. The sky outside was a crazy translucent pink. The birds suddenly went from silent to having a million important bird conversations at the top of their voices. The streets were totally empty of humans, though.

Eventually I gave up on falling back to sleep, had some breakfast and settled on my bed with a notebook. I was excited to have a maths question to think about all on my own. Solving the first one in front of Ty had been a huge rush. I mean sure, some of that was down to Ty watching me do it, his long fingers tip-tapping musically on his leg. But some of it – most of it, I swear – was that feeling that you've really understood something. With maths, I find that it's like learning to ride a bike, or swim. Once I've understood, I have it forever. It's not like writing an essay or drawing a picture, where I might get better but each one is a whole new challenge. Maths is like... I don't know, like exploring a dense forest, cutting a clear path as you go. Everything behind you stays clear and easy to walk around. You can even build a house there, make a pretty garden, plant some new flowers. As long as you tend to it, it won't grow back dense and muddled again. And... that's enough of that metaphor.

All this to say that I was in a great mood when I sat down cross-legged on my bed, my favourite studying position, with a handful of the fancy ginger biscuits Mum gets from her favourite store on the Heath. The thing is, though, that it didn't happen the same *at all* this time: no sudden realisation or cogs in my brain clicking into place. Instead, I thought and thought until I was cross-eyed, and got exactly nowhere.

The question was:

> **Question 349:** How many people do you need to have in a room to get at least a 50% chance that two of them share the same birthday?

I started out how I always do with these problems, trying to find a pattern:

First, I calculated the probability that in a room with just two people, they share a birthday. That was pretty easy – if you called them Abby and Ben: Abby's birthday could be any day of the year, but then for the birthdays to match, Ben only had one possibility for his birthday: it had to be the same day as Abby's. So, forgetting about leap years, Abby had all 365 days possible out of the 365 days of the year for her birthday, and Ben had only 1 day possible out of the 365 days of the year for his birthday.

The probability that they had the same birthday was therefore 365/365x1/365, which is tiny – about 0.0027.

Then I tried to think about the possibility that in a room with three people, two or more of them shared a birthday. This was already way harder! There were quite a few possibilities to consider: Abby and Ben might have the same birthday, or Abby and Cassandra, or Ben and Cassandra, or all three of them could have the same birthday. I worked it out methodically and came up with another tiny probability, just a little bit bigger than the one for Abby and Ben, and still very far from the 50% I was trying to get to.

When I tried to do the calculation for Abby, Ben, Cassandra and Deepak, things went badly. I tried the calculation three times because I kept forgetting some of the cases. Abby and Ben could have the same birthday, but then Cassandra and Deepak might or might not have the same birthday, or three of them could have the same birthday and not the fourth, or all four... In any case, I tried it three times and got three different answers, all of which were still tiny.

This was clearly not the way to go. I couldn't see any pattern, and attempting the straight calculation for 10, or 20, or 100, or 183 people (my first guess) was completely out of the question.

Every other idea I tried came to the same messy conclusion that I had no idea what I was doing, until I was all out. I filled my notebook with scribbles, tore out the useless pages and crumpled them angrily, and even threw them across the room in a bad moment, which gave me approximately three seconds of calm before I wanted to scream again. Then I flopped despondently on my bed and did some major procrastination – watched groups of kids playing outside, scrolled through TikTok, looked up the news, looked up memes about the news, watched some *Freaks & Geeks* on Youtube... all of it far more appealing than butting my head against that stupid problem.

Finally, I gave up and switched to doing my actual homework instead. It was pretty calming, going through a list of maths questions that I had been given all the tools for, ticking them off one by one. I felt myself go back to normal.

No wonder some people hate maths. If you're trying to work out the answer to a question when you haven't properly understood it, it's the most awful feeling. I'd never experienced it before, really. Until now, if I ever got stuck on a problem, I could just go over my notes carefully and it would fall into place. But this – this was frustrating and miserable. No one should ever have to feel like this at school.

I finished my homework feeling a lot better. I checked my phone, which I had been avoiding really hard all day. I kept wanting to tell M everything that had happened with Ty, so I felt that the easiest way to deal with this was just to not look at my phone at all – we all know that ignoring things totally works.

Unfortunately, when I did look at it, I had a text from M reminding me that we had plans to go to her friends' party tonight. I texted back to tell her I wasn't up for it. I was really not in the mood for a party, what with this stupid maths question I had to work on, which was the only way we could disband the international drug ring that Oli was laundering money for (yes, I watch too much Netflix). I decided I would much rather sleep lots and feel ready to think about it again fresh tomorrow.

M refuses to have a smartphone, instead she uses an old flip phone which means you can't tell if she's seen your message and she doesn't get emojis which is very inconvenient. She's always borrowing *my* phone to post on her Instagram account @presentedw_ocomment, which is photos of sexist or racist or otherwise -ist stuff she comes across that she posts without, you know, comment. Like a sign that says *wife* with an arrow pointing away from a pub and *whisky* with an arrow pointing inside it, or that time our school made a poster in support of BLM with a picture of only white staff members. She's recently reached 10k followers, which seems to be the number where you start getting spammed with offers to promote exciting things such as diet tea and foot peels.

I waited for a few minutes, but she didn't answer. I definitely wasn't emotionally ready to get back to Oli's question and downstairs Emma and Mum seemed to be locked in a screaming match. I put Spotify on, but my Discover Weekly list is stuck on French indie bands and it couldn't compete with the sound.

Seriously, Emma is only eight – you'd think we'd have had a few more years of sweet angelic child before this behaviour. Or it could happen never – I mean, just look at me, I'm weathering the teenage years with gracefulness and ease and she does share an estimated 25% of my genes.

I decided to go over to see Dad, who had sent me a very enticing photo of a pitcher of lemonade. The weather is pretending it's Italy today, and Dad's garden gets the sun right up until the last rays (Mum's is a morning-sun garden, which is no use to me at all).

Dad greeted me by saying that my hair was too short (M cut it for me on Wednesday to about chin length) but then that's one of the only two things he ever says about my hair (the other one being 'it's nice'). He and I drank the whole pitcher of lemonade while he ran me through the new autumn menu at his restaurant, which I haven't tasted yet. He told me about the famous people who have come in recently (Keira Knightley, some rugby players I don't know, a young guy that Dad was convinced was from 'that show you like', but he was unable to describe the show or the guy so it will remain a mystery). It was very relaxing, especially after a few nights of Mum obsessively talking about my uni applications, and made me forget a bit about all the recent drama.

I'm still here now, writing on a lounger outside, while Dad is inside listening to The Gypsy Kings with the windows open, like every other dad in the world.

He went inside to apply his professional chef skills to making us a superior quality snack, but now I can hear him talking. His voice is wafting out of the windows, over the sound of the music. He's been on the phone for about fifteen times longer than he ever is when he's talking to me and he keeps wandering out and blushing and then going back inside to hide.

Dad and I never talk about any woman (women?) he might have in his life; never *once* have we broached the subject.

My parents had a very calm divorce that people think sounds like total science fiction. There was a very short moment of not calm, right at the beginning. I was only eight, but I do remember some drinking and late-night shouting on the phone after Mum told Dad she was leaving, and like a week later she had moved into a house on the very same street with another guy. Then Emma was born eight months after that and, well, you don't need to be good at maths to know what that means.

But, unbelievably, Emma's birth didn't make Dad more angry at all. Instead he calmed all the way down, hand delivered some extremely cute baby clothes, did the whole kissing Mum on the cheek and shaking John's hand and standing in the doorway with his legs apart being all manly. Then little by little he even started staying for tea or even dinner when he came by to drop me off. Of course, that stopped a couple of years later when I was deemed old enough to walk between the houses on my own, but he still gets a birthday present every year for Emma and calls John when he needs money advice and generally behaves like we're all a big happy family. His own private life, however, remains a mystery.

So naturally, I'm pretty intrigued by the phone call. It's funny watching Dad acting all secretive and giggly. But what he doesn't know is that when he's talking in his bedroom with the window open like this, I can hear him very clearly.

'Yes, she's here,' he's saying to someone. 'No, she's in the garden. She can't hear me, don't worry.' I laugh silently and eavesdrop a bit harder. 'I'll see you on Tuesday. Come and get me at the restaurant around 4? Yes? Ok, that's perfect.' A pause. 'I can't wait. Bye, Rachie.'

Wait – Rachie? RACHEL? He's talking to *Mum*??

***

Ok – I took a break to digest the news, and now we're back. I've turned the idea round and round in my head. First of all, I didn't even have any clue that my parents were talking on the phone with any kind of regularity. Could this call have been about something perfectly innocent? Discussing their shared offspring, perhaps? But no, the topic of yours truly came up, only to be dismissed. The schoolboy voice was there. The words, 'I can't wait' were pronounced. There is only one explanation possible, isn't there?

I called M, who was totally ecstatic. 'That's so amazing! It's awesome! It's like a fairytale! They're going back to their true love. They can get married again! You could be best kid and wear a suit like Rory in *Gilmore Girls*.'

Of course M would get excited about this. She doesn't know who her dad is and she is really into parental romance – *The Parent Trap* is basically a sacred text to her. But hearing her so excited, I realised that I'm not excited myself. Sure, I dreamed about it a lot when I was younger, but now? I remember how much they argued at the end. It was awful – they really knew how to hurt each other. Mum would heat up a sad dinner from the Sainsbury's low-calorie range rather than eat the food Dad had prepared, Dad would tell her that she was behaving like her mother… They're happier now, they really are. And there's Emma to think of too, she doesn't deserve to be a product of a broken home like me. Plus, given her personality, she would end up with all the long-term, divorced-parents traumas that I have clearly avoided.

I told M that I didn't share her enthusiasm, but she was confident that her reaction was the correct one, not mine. Then she convinced me to go to the party tonight – of course she did.

I hung up and lay back down on the chair, mentally preparing myself. The party is at one of M's primary-school friends' place. Her group from primary school are all still friends and go to the same secondary school now – M is the only one who switched. I've met them all a few times, but they do not seem to find me particularly memorable.

Dad has just come back out and pulled up a chair next to mine in the sun. He's reading the paper. He looks up at me. 'Hey, aren't those my sunglasses?' They are, actually, but I shake my head *no*. He smiles and goes back to his paper, looking completely like he hasn't just made a highly suspicious phone call at all.

Sunday 9th October

I'm still in bed even though it is technically no longer morning. I really don't feel like getting up. Oli's question is waiting for me when I do, which is not an invigorating thought. Ty has been sending me sweet, encouraging messages, but I imagine what he really means is, *you must find the solution before my brother inadvertently starts a world war by hacking into the US military's communication system.*

Also, last night was not the best, which is not helping with the getting out of bed part.

I left Dad's after dinner and got the bus to the address M had given me, which was in Hackney. I rang the doorbell and eventually someone opened the door. I immediately regretted not having made an effort with my outfit, because everyone looked incredible. The guy who'd opened the door for me wandered away once he realised he didn't know me. I scanned the room and I was very happy to see that M was already there.

'This is Rowan,' she said as I walked over. 'It's their party. Rowan, this is Clara.'

Rowan was wearing a very sharply cut three-piece suit and looked like David Bowie. 'Hi Clara, welcome, welcome! Meet my boyfriend, Max!'

'Rowan and Max are like the parents of the group,' M said. 'They make sure we're always entertained and watered.' She jiggled a full bottle of vodka in her hand. 'Speaking of which,' she added, 'I still haven't opened this.'

'Mixers over there, darling!' Max said, pointing to the kitchen through the side door. He was wearing a tight black top with a hood and wide brown velvet trousers. M was just in dark jeans and a transparent white tank, but of course she looked like a vision. I felt a nervous squeeze watching her walk away with the vodka.

'Give me a hug, sweetie. I always do this the first time I meet someone,' Max said. 'Just come right in here and breathe with me.'

I put my arms around him and breathed in and out. I wasn't sure if I was meant to stop at any point.

'There you go!' he announced suddenly, and stepped back. I wondered if he now knew all my secrets, which would actually have been a relief. But it seemed not. 'Make yourself at home sweetie!' he said brightly, then he turned around and walked away.

I surveyed the surroundings. We were in a bare room with a table pushed against the back wall and a broken sofa on one side, which about ten people were perched on. There were another ten or so standing around and drinking. No one was dancing, but they were all vaping. I walked into the kitchen to get a drink. M was in a group with a boy who was staring at her as if she was made out of caramel and a girl with a shaved head. She and the girl were ignoring the guy entirely and having a very animated discussion. It looked like they were arguing, but actually they were aggressively agreeing with each other.

'Can you believe they are taxed as a *luxury item*?! Oh yes, what luxury, stuffing my vagina full of harmful substances! Oh yes, make me pay extra for that sweet sweet toxic shock syndrome!'

'I'll come sit on your sofa when I'm on my period and *then* you can decide if they really are a luxury item!'

I rinsed a mug in the sink, poured vodka in it and then some cranberry juice from an open carton. I went exploring upstairs – it turned out that by climbing out of the bedroom window you could get onto the roof. There were another dozen people up there. I walked round a chimney and saw a couple intensely making out, both with a hand down the other's pants.

I scrambled past them and behind another chimney. There was just one guy there, smoking weed on his own. I sat down next to him and he passed me the joint without saying a word, which turned out to be so strong that my head immediately started spinning right off my neck.

Me: Whoa.

Him: [nodding, looking proud of himself] From Afghanistan. Hey, I know you, right? You're M's friend?

Me: Yeah. You're Dylan.

Dylan: How beautiful is this? [he gestured towards the view. It was actually weirdly wonderful, a tangle of houses and roads, some windows glowing and some dark, and the pinpricks of car headlights creeping along.]

Dylan: So tell me, what is your life plan, M's friend?

Me: Well, um, my name is Clara, actually. And I don't know, I guess go to university next year and then I'll see—

Dylan: University! So what, you buy into all that bullshit? Like everyone needs an e-du-ca-tion?

Me: I don't know about everyone, but yeah, I want to—

Dylan: Uni is just how the government brainwashes us all. Don't give in to them! You gotta live! You gotta make art! You gotta make music! Actually, I'm in a band, you should check us out... We don't have a name yet. The Band With No Name.

Me: How can I find you then?

Dylan: You can't *find* us, you have to *know* us. I'll send you the info, M's friend.

Me: [at this point I got up to leave] Clara.

Dylan offered me the weed again, oblivious to my mood, and waved at me when I declined. I climbed back past the two chimneys, where the couple were still going at it, and down the stairs, really not feeling it.

I'd come here because I didn't want M to think I was acting strangely with her, but she was off talking to other people. I really wanted to just go home and go to bed. I figured I could leave and no one would notice, but M was in the middle of the dancefloor and spotted me. She grabbed my arm.

'You have that face on,' she said. 'What happened?'

'Nothing, I'm just not in the mood M, I should go...'

'Oh no, please stay! Listen, it's our song!'

I laughed. It's the line we use if one of us is talking to a boy we don't want to, to extricate ourselves. A Drake song was playing, *One Dance*. Not the worst choice in the world, I guess.

'I'm just feeling really lame,' I said. 'I hate my outfit, everyone else looks so good...' *and the only think I can think about is this thing I can't tell you,* I added in my head.

'You look amazing! Minimalist. Domino was just saying she's obsessed with you.'

'Really?'

'Yeah. I mean, she's obsessed with your haircut, which *is* my creation... Domino!' she called. 'Come over here and tell Clara what you said to me!'

The girl with the shaved head walked over, winking, and just at that moment *Gold Digger* came on and everyone started dancing. The guy playing YouTube DJ raised both his arms in self-congratulation.

We danced for a bit and I started thinking that coming had been a good idea after all, but then M got her laser eyes going and leaned towards me. She'd obviously been drinking her drinks at a much higher rate than me. 'So now tell me for real... what's going *on* with you?' she said unsteadily.

'Nothing is going on,' I said, looking at the floor.

She squinted. 'Come on,' she whined.

Of course she'd realised I was hiding something – she has a superhuman nose for that kind of thing. How could I ever have convinced myself that she wouldn't notice me lying to her?

She took another sip of her drink and shook her head. 'Fine then, don't tell me.' She kept dancing, but she had a sullen look on her face.

I left not long after. I felt a bit sick about M, but Ty had only told me about his brother two days before and I'd like to think of myself as a more-than-48-hour secret-keeper.

I called Sam even though it was late. I missed him. Suddenly I really didn't feel like having secrets and mysteries to solve, I just felt like life going back to how it was last year. He picked up and said hello in a groggy, sleepy voice, and we talked the whole time until I got home.

Sunday 9th October – afternoon

After writing this morning I finally got myself out of bed and delayed getting back to thinking about Oli's question by scrolling through all of Instagram, exiting my room as slowly as possible, eating my granola one cluster at a time and chewing each one conscientiously, hand-squeezing some oranges, and listening to Emma's very long-winded story about her classmates, all of whom seem to be named after fruit.

Mum suggested I go with her to the supermarket and I was *almost* tempted, so great was my mission to procrastinate, but not quite tempted enough. Instead, I took off the faded T-shirt of Dads's that I sleep in, wrapped myself in a towel and headed off to take what I intended to be a record-length shower. Only I'd barely got going on the shampoo when a brainwave hit me. I rinsed off in a hurry and rushed back to my bedroom.

It was a trick for probabilities that Mr Howard has often told us about – I couldn't believe I hadn't thought about it earlier. Sometimes, he explained, it's much easier to calculate the probability of the *opposite* statement to the one you want.

When you do that, you are also calculating the probability you want, because:

the probability of something + the probability of its opposite = 1 (or 100%).

And so:

the probability you want = 1 – the probability of its opposite.

So in our case, where we were considering an event with a probability of over 50%, its opposite would have a probability of under 50%.

The time when it's useful to consider using this trick is exactly what was happening to me: when you're getting confused with your calculations because the event you are considering is convoluted with lots of different situations that you need to factor in. In cases like this, the opposite event is often much simpler to think about. Which I guess makes sense, that if something is turning out to be too complex then you should try its opposite (is that a metaphor for life or something?)

Anyway, Oli's birthday question was exactly right for this trick, because the opposite of: *at least two people in the room have the same birthday* is: *none of the people in the room have the same birthday* – a much simpler situation to think about, since you don't need to consider all the different possibilities for birthday matches (like only two people having the same birthday and no one else, or two people one one day and two people on another, or three people all on the same day...)

So the question became:

> **Question 349*:** How many people do you need to put in a room for the probability that none of them share a birthday to be less than 50%?

Then, I did my usual technique of starting right at the beginning and building up, to spot the pattern.

One person in the room - if it was just Abby by herself in a room, no one else had the same birthday as her since no one else was even there, so the probability that no two people in the room shared a birthday was 1.

Two people in the room - if Abby and Ben were in a room together:

- Abby could have her birthday on any day of the year, so 365 possible days out of the 365 days in the year;
- Ben could have his birthday on any day except Abby's, so he had 364 possible days for his birthday out of 365 days in the year.

This meant that the probability that they didn't share a birthday was 365/365x364/365, which was around 0.997 – much too big.

Three people in the room - if we had Abby, Ben and Cassandra together:

- Abby could have her birthday on any day of the year - 365 possible days out of the 365 days in the year;
- Ben had every day of the year available for his birthday except for Abby's birthday – 364 possible days out of 365;
- Cassandra had every day of the year available for her birthday, except for Abby's birthday and Ben's birthday - 363 possible days out of 365.

So the probability that no two of them shared a birthday was 365/365x364/365x363/365, which was around 0.992 – still much too big.

Four people in the room - if we had Abby, Ben, Cassandra and Deepak:

- Abby could have her birthday on any day of the year - 365 possible days out of the 365 days in the year;
- Ben had every day of the year available for his birthday except for Abby's birthday – 364 possible days out of 365;
- Cassandra had every day of the year available for her birthday, except for Abby's birthday and Ben's birthday - 363 possible days out of 365.
- Deepak had every day of the year available for his birthday, except for Abby, Ben and Cassandra's birthdays – 362 possible days out of 365.

So the probability that no two of them shared a birthday was 365/365x364/365x363/365x362/365, which was around 0.984.

The probability was still much too big, but this time the pattern was clear! Every time you added a new person to the room, they could have any birthday apart from the birthdays of all the people that were already in the room. So I just needed to keep going from my probability for 4 people in the room, multiply by 361/365 for the fifth person, then by 360/365 for the sixth person, and then 359/365 for the seventh person, and so on, until I found the first person who made the probability go below 0.5.

I did so with some trepidation, as I did not fancy having to keep going until I'd done it for around 183 people. But pretty soon the probability was getting smaller and smaller, and I reached the magic number a lot sooner than I expected: it was just 23.

When you had 23 people in a room, the probability that none of them shared a birthday was 365/365x364/365x363/365x362/365x... all the way until ...x343/365. And this came out to around 0.493, the first probability below 0.5.

I let myself fall onto my pillows. In terms of how great I felt, this ranked higher than a girl on the Tube complimenting my outfit or getting the answer to a question on University Challenge before the contestants (though probably still below that time I overheard Dad bragging about me at a dinner when he thought I was in a different room). Yesterday's frustrations were completely forgotten.

I gave myself a couple of minutes to enjoy the feeling and texted Ty to tell him I had the answer. I also had a message from M in response to my earlier text saying sorry for leaving the party early, so I figured that she must have forgiven me, or even forgotten our conversation entirely due to extreme drunkenness, which added to my great mood. M wasn't mad at me! We'd find Oli before the Chinese spies whose message he'd intercepted! I took my excitement downstairs to start prepping for tonight's cake.

Sunday is cake-for-dinner day – the true sign of Mum's genius, if you ask me. We rotate who gets to choose the cake every week and this time was Emma's choice. It's quite predictable: Mum likes chocolate, coffee and bitter stuff like marmalade. I like nuts and caramel. Emma likes vanilla and sugary sugar. You could say it's just an age thing, but I've *never* had as unsophisticated a palate as Emma; I've always liked the same stuff. Anyway, while we switch who gets to pick the recipe, I'm always the head chef. Mum doesn't like cooking very much (though she's pretty good at it – learned a few things from Dad I guess) plus the one time she agreed to do it, she picked a healthy recipe which used apple compote instead of butter, and that just goes against the whole cake-for-dinner ethos. Emma's personality is not at all suited to baking, as the mere concept of measuring out ingredients seems to offend her. So, me it is! Emma hadn't given me a specific recipe, only decreed that it had to be huuuuuge and pink, with flowers.

Mum was downstairs, and I sent her out to pick flowers from the garden, seeing as there was no way I was going to waste energy making frosting flowers only for Emma to lick them straight off the cake as she always does. I flipped through some of Mum's old cookbooks. She never uses them anymore, but they are crinkled and stained from years ago and they open straight at her old favourite recipes – upside-down orange and polenta cake, and salads from when the western world first heard about quinoa.

I found a classic vanilla sponge recipe in a satisfyingly old-fashioned-looking volume and started making the batter. My plan was to bake three cakes and slice each of them into three thin layers, to make a nine-layer extravaganza complete with raspberries, strawberries and lemon cream in between each layer and some pink frosting for decoration and Emma's happiness. Obviously, I was riding high on my mathematical success.

Mum came back from the garden with a beautiful bunch of wild flowers of all sorts of colours. They looked very pretty together because Mum has a secret flower-arranging talent. She set them in a glass of water to be ready for later and then she spotted the cookbook I was using.

'Oh my god,' she practically squealed, and picked it up to flip through the pages. She found the one she was looking for. 'This was the cookbook of a very popular food magazine that doesn't exist anymore. They published a volume every December with that year's best recipes, plus a few extras and, at the end, a section for reader-suggested recipes... Look!'

I peered at the words she was pointing to.

Rachel's chocolate truffles... with coffee!
Suggested by Justin Valentine.

'Wow,' I said. 'That's pretty cute.'

'Yeah...' Mum said dreamily.

'You were already a chocolate-and-coffee person.'

'Since the day I was born, baby. Your dad and my wedding cake was coffee and chocolate. Fruit cake was out of the question.'

I started. Just yesterday I'd overheard Dad on the phone, and now here was Mum looking about as nostalgic as the old narrator guy in *The Notebook*. They had a traditional fruit cake at her wedding with John, I remember. They had everything traditional, to please John's family, with everyone studiously ignoring the fact that there was a toddler-sized problem with the whole story. Actually – I know that the photo John's parents display in their house is one where Emma had been conveniently whipped away.

'Show me the photos again,' I said to Mum. Nothing like looking at old photos to get the stories going.

She climbed up to her bedroom and returned with an old album. 'Look at this one,' she kept saying, delightedly pointing at family members' freakishly fresh faces.

'Wow, Dad had *so much* hair.'

'Yeah, hard to believe, isn't it?' Mum giggled.

She turned the page and there it was: the picture of them dancing, the flowers slipping from Mum's hair, both of them laughing. She was wearing a very simple slip dress, with what she always refers to as a *daringly low* back, which she'd managed to keep hidden from her mother until the day of, when Grams could do nothing that Mum hadn't emotionally prepared for. 'You're in this photo too, you know.' She winked at me.

'What? You never told me that! You said I was born premature!'

'Yeah, well,' she shrugged. 'That's what we told everyone. That you'd been conceived on the wedding night and born early.' I wrinkled my nose at her. 'Thankfully, you were a small baby, only 5lb2. But you were born right on time.'

'Would Grams have been really angry?'

'Oh my god, yes. You can't ever tell her, of course.'

'Mum. Of course, I have no intention of telling Grams that kind of thing.'

'Well, you have a different relationship with her than I do. You can do no wrong in her eyes, you know that. Just don't get all cosy with her one day and spill my secrets.'

I shook my head.

Mum looked back at the photo, tracing the contours of her dress with her finger. 'When we were married, all I ever heard from her was, "Justin is irresponsible, you can't sustain a relationship with those working hours, you can't have a family..." They could argue about literally everything, from socialism to how to make scrambled eggs. She used to say, "making food for other people isn't a profession – if it was, every woman of my generation should be called a chef!" Of course, now she acts like she always thought he was the most wonderful man in the world, and I made a terrible mistake by leaving him.' She half-smiled. 'You know, a part of me will always love your father. When you leave someone, you don't stop loving them...'

I waited for more with bated breath, but my phone chose that instant to beep extra loudly. It was a message from Ty: *Can you come over now? My parents are out tonight.*

Jolted out of her expansive state, Mum snapped the photo album shut and disappeared upstairs to put it away. There was no way I'd get anything more out of her now. I hunted down our three matching cake tins in a rush. I'm not sure how it happens but they're never where I expect them to be. I do not think that Mum and I have the same vision for sorting out kitchen equipment. We also don't have the same vision for tidying my room but that is another matter.

I divided up the batter equally between the three tins, put them in the oven, set the timer, and wrote instructions for Mum on what to do when they were done – ready for me to finish them off when I got back from Ty's.

I went to my room to get changed into my magic pair of Adidas trousers that say I-just-pulled-these-on, but somehow make my ass look 20% more Kardashian-y. At the last minute I decided to put mascara on – of course I blinked too quickly and made a black smear across my cheek that I then had to sort out.

I rushed out of the house and practically ran all the way. When I got there, Ty opened the door. He was wearing faded brown carpenter jeans and a green T-shirt, and his hair was a bit damp. We ran up the stairs to his flat and down the corridor to his room. As soon as I walked in, I spotted that the photo of

Ty and Alice had gone. My heart started beating super quickly. *Stop it*, I told myself, *it doesn't mean anything.*

I turned my attention to the computer, which was already on Ty's bed, turned on and waiting for us. I punched in the answer and crossed my fingers. Again, the pixelated tick, and that burning split-second of wondering what would happen next. But then, it was just another question.

We looked at each other, dismayed. How many of these would there be?

I turned my attention back to the screen and read carefully:

Question 266: Decode the RSA-encoded message 90 encrypted with the public key $(247,11)$.

One glance at the question was enough to tell me there was no way I could do it – I didn't know what RSA even meant or stood for. I thought of Oli (who I imagined as Ty with a few forehead wrinkles and skinnier because of the whole computer-instead-of-football thing). How many questions would he expect us to do?

'I don't know what any of this means,' I said to Ty regretfully. I really wanted to see his Christmas eyes light up when I got the answer again.

'Wait!' he blurted out. 'Come with me.'

I followed him to the bedroom across the hallway, Oli's old room. It looked very much like Ty's, except the walls were bare and it overlooked the street, not the garden. It was being used to store a few boxes, and two bicycles.

Ty stepped over the mess and went to the bookshelf. He read through the titles rapidly, his finger running along the top of the books. Then he stopped and pulled one out. 'Oli was obsessed with codebreakers for a while,' Ty said, handing the book to me. *The Code Book* by Simon Singh. 'He idolized Simon Singh when he was younger. Look – it's signed.' Ty opened the front cover to show me Singh's double-S scrawl. 'He taught me one of the codes when we were kids and we used it to write secret messages to each other. I was so slow at it – it would take me ages to decode his stuff and he only used to write messages like *your hair looks terrible today.*' he rolled his eyes.

'What code was it?' I asked.

'Nothing to do with the question unfortunately. It's called the one-time pad code, and there is no public key. The whole way the one-time pad code works is that you have a *private* key, which is just a random list of letters that you can't show anyone else. You know it's funny – Oli liked that code because it was so low-tech. Unlike all the codes that are built on rules and algorithms, this code is totally unbreakable for someone who doesn't have the key. Spies used to carry the key along with them but in totally hidden ways, like a tiny onion-skin paper that you needed a magnifying glass to read. Oli just loved that. He's the same with everything. In his life outside work he barely uses computers. He doesn't even have a smartphone, just an old Nokia.'

'That *is* funny,' I said. 'Like M.'

I took the book from him and scanned the table of contents, but nothing jumped out at me. Ty looked at me expectantly. I wanted so badly to come up with the answer then and there, but I swallowed my pride.

'Ty, I think I need to take this home and work on it by myself again.'

'Oh, yes, of course, of course,' he said, shaking his head. 'Sorry I'm breathing down your neck. That's definitely the best way to make anyone forget how to do maths.'

I laughed nervously. The idea of Ty breathing down my neck made my spine all tingly. I looked back on the shelf to distract myself. 'So, Oli likes science fiction, huh?' I said.

'Yeah, it's pretty much the only thing he reads. I've tried to give him other books but...' he shrugged.

'Apart from *Lady Chatterley's Lover*,' I pointed out.

Ty laughed. 'Not even that. He got by on CliffsNotes.'

'I haven't really read any science fiction,' I said. 'M loves Ursula Le Guin.'

'Oli has lots of hers. But his favourite is this one.' He pulled it off the shelf. 'Do you want it? It might be a good introduction to sci-fi, if you're interested.'

I looked at the book. The cover was a beautiful orange illustration of what looked like a desert. The book was *Dune* by Frank Herbert. 'Oh yes,' I said, 'there's a film.'

'Yeah,' Ty said. 'Two films even. There's one from the '80s too.'

'Yes please, I'll borrow it. Thanks,' I said. I figured that maybe reading Oli's favourite book would help me get to know him, seeing as I couldn't talk to him.

'No problem. Hey... do you want to stay for dinner? I definitely owe you sustenance,' Ty suggested.

'Yes!' I nearly shouted. 'I mean, yeah, ok.'

What was I doing? This was hardly the way to keep my distance.

I followed Ty into the kitchen where he chopped up an onion and some garlic, which made my eyes puff and tear up while he seemed entirely unaffected.

He handed me a tissue, and I went to wash my face in the bathroom and survey the damage. It was not good – my red-rimmed eyes were also smeared with mascara. I cleaned up, had a quick funeral for any thought of Ty ever fancying me and returned to the kitchen.

Ty was frying an array of spices in some ghee, having also chopped a few peppers, opened a can of chickpeas and set the rice cooker on. It smelled totally incredible, and I realised I was starving. 'So you know how to cook!' I said.

'Yes. Well, only Indian food. My grandma – my mum's mum – has been teaching me. She never taught my mum. At the time, my grandparents were so intent on raising their children to fit in here that they forgot to keep some of the traditions going. Mum makes a great fish pie and the best Yorkshire puddings, but she orders curry from a restaurant.'

'And your grandmother decided to teach you instead?'

'Yeah,' he shrugged. 'Mum is now old and unteachable. She failed to produce any daughters, and Oli wasn't interested so... I was the last resort.'

'My dad is a chef. He has his own restaurant, actually.'

'That's amazing! Has he taught *you* to cook?'

'He's tried. He lets me assist him sometimes. At home, I mean. Not at work. Don't worry – it's safe to eat there.'

Ty laughed graciously. 'Whenever I make something with my grandmother, she tastes it like this.' He smacked his lips a few times, eyes closed. 'And then she always shrugs with disappointment and says, "it's ok, we can eat it".'

'My dad does exactly the same! He says, "not bad, I suppose", and then makes a little face.'

'It's like, *you're* the one teaching *me*! I'm not responsible if it's not as good as yours!'

'Well, at least I'm glad I'm not the only family disappointment around,' I said.

Ty laughed again, and I felt something flutter in my chest. I had made him laugh, like a few times in a row!

He set the food on a couple of plates. 'So,' he said as he sat down, 'can you handle spicy food?' He raised one eyebrow at me. The flutters returned, somewhat lower down this time.

'Just you watch,' I said cockily and shoved a big forkful in my mouth. It was absolutely delicious, and didn't taste like any curry I've ever had in a restaurant. There were layers and layers of flavours and then, at the end, a searing heat. I smiled through it and blinked back tears. 'It's amazing,' I said with fake nonchalance, once the heat had died down.

'Well, I'm impressed,' he nodded.

The evening went by in a flash. Ty asked me to explain the birthday question to him. He was very disbelieving of the fact that you only need 23 people in a room to get a 50% chance of a shared birthday.

'You know what I think is even more counter-intuitive?' I said, 'When you have just 50 people, the probability climbs up to over 95%.'

'No way,' he shook his head. 'There are 365 days in the year, that's... so much more than 50! How is it possible?'

'It's just what the maths says, you can calculate it yourself.'

'But it *can't* be possible!'

I shrugged and Ty laughed.

'I have exactly this type of conversation with Oli. He doesn't understand what I mean when I say that I find something counter-intuitive. He always says: "but I've shown you *why* it's true, what does intuition have to do with it?"'

'Well, I'm not quite as scientifically minded as that. I definitely agree with you about the birthday problem, even if I calculated it myself. It still somehow feels like it can't be true.'

'Is maths your favourite subject?' Ty asked.

'Yes, it is. That's what I want to study at uni. I really hope I get into Cambridge,' I told him. (Though I didn't mention how Mum has a whole album at home that consists of pictures of me in every single college in Cambridge because we wanted to decide which one seemed like the best fit – I'm applying to Gonville & Caius, my top choice; Emmanuel was Mum's, by the way.)

'Oh wow! So you're doing your application soon, aren't you?'

'Don't remind me,' I groaned. 'Less than a week. Nothing is ready.'

'That's very cool in any case. I'm sure you'll get in. I want to do English, I hope at UCL.' I must have looked a bit dubious because he quickly added, 'You don't need to be good at maths to apply for English, you know. I actually get good grades in my other three subjects.'

'Sorry,' I said, feeling bad and judgy.

'So, you know, don't hesitate if someone you know encodes a computer with questions about Shakespeare plays. I'm your man.' He winked.

Suddenly his phone beeped. Ty looked at it and frowned.

'What is it?' I asked.

'Oh...' he shook his head. 'My mum asked me earlier if I'd heard from Oli lately,' he said. 'Apparently, he hasn't been answering her messages either, which is weird. And now she just told me that she went by his flat and saw that he's not been there. Why wouldn't he answer her? I understand if he's ignoring me, but surely he realises that not answering our mum will get her anxious.'

'Does he ever go off on his own like that?'

'Yes,' Ty said slowly. 'He does, but... his phone is actually off now. It goes straight to voicemail when you call. That's not unheard of either though, if he's really into a project he'll turn it off to avoid distractions, but it's been several days.' He sighed. 'I told my mum that I *had* heard from him recently. Do you think that was a mistake? I didn't want her to start wondering what he was up to, because of what he said in the note. But what if something's happened?' He shook his head and answered his own question. 'Sorry, I'm overreacting. Oli only answers his messages when he feels like it anyway. This probably means nothing.'

He smiled at me, but he was obviously worried. I felt worried too. I'd been constructing stupid scenarios in my head, but this was real life, and we had no idea what was going on. It was a lot scarier.

When I eventually left it was past 10pm, which meant I had been there for more than four hours. It felt like about thirteen minutes: no awkward silences, no awkward moments apart from the ones I've already recounted (a reasonable number, I think?) So now it's official, not only do I find him TASTY, I actually really like him too. This is not going according to plan.

I hadn't checked my phone all evening. There were five missed calls from M, and some from Mum as well as a message requesting that I confirm I was alive and a photo of the cake (they'd messed the presentation up totally, which was a blow, though Mum claimed it was still delicious). I texted Mum *sorry* and I called M, but there was no answer.

There were only three other people in the bus, and we each sat in our own row, not making eye contact. I looked up *Dune* on my phone and was reminded that the movie had Timothée Chalamet as the lead, so that definitely piqued my interest. I opened up the book and got engrossed right away, even though I think I understood only about half of what was happening. There's the son of a duke called Paul (Timmy!) who has prescient visions, a planet made out of desert with a native people called the Fremen who hate the current rulers, and an addictive drug that enhances mental capacities. No robots, computers or AI though. Just like using an old mobile phone and preferring codes that rely on paper. I guess that when you know as much about technology as Oli does, it becomes too boring. Or too scary.

| 3 |

RSA Encryption

Monday 10th October

Mondays are the worst days. I know some people say the title goes to Wednesdays, and I guess others would nominate Sundays because of the scaries, but they are wrong. Nothing beats the alarm ringing on Monday morning, throwing you into the week with no regard to the fact that you've unlearnt all of the expected behaviours and coping mechanisms and appropriate sleeping schedule over the weekend. (There, I hope you are satisfied with these philosophical thoughts, since the rest of today's entry will be free of anything useful.)

I was even later than usual this morning, having passed out into a deep slumber that my alarm was no match for. I ran the whole way to school. Ok, who am I kidding? I ran two minutes in the direction of school and panted the rest of my way there with a bad stitch in my side, sliding through the hall doors and making it to assembly with five seconds to spare. I spotted Ty on the other side of the room next to Alice who looked, as ever, perfect in her low ponytail and jumpsuit from the French brands section of Selfridge's.

Ty's eyes crossed mine and he gave me a smile which filled me with jitters. He was wearing a light-blue long-sleeve T-shirt that still had creases from being folded in the shop. M was nowhere to be found – she was going to be in so much trouble.

Assembly was about the importance of revising during half-term. Everyone's mood dropped by a few degrees. I saw Ty get his phone out and then my phone beeped. *The official position is that working on my brother's stuff counts as revision,* he'd written. I laughed.

Next to Ty, Alice was frowning. I took a big breath and put them out of my head. By the time the bell rang, there was still no sign of M. I frowned and checked my phone, but there was nothing. *Where are you?* I texted her. She answered right away: *Not feeling great so stayed home.*

On one hand, this meant that she wasn't dead in a ditch. M is a big fan of staying home from school – she probably misses about half of the days when she has her period, writing delightfully gory excuse notes for herself that Amanda happily signs. But on the other, much-grippier hand, she always lets me know when she's not coming and sends me relentless updates on how she is enjoying her free time while I am at school. Really, M has two modes: either she's completely happy and everything is great, or she's deathly angry or upset and I know why in the tiniest little details (whether it's directed at me or not). But this written-by-a-bot-sounding message – I've never known her like this before. She never called me back last night either, after all those missed calls.

I texted her the lobster emoji. I missed her. School is boring when she isn't around. That's what the lobster meant – *I miss you*. Of course, her stupid phone wouldn't show the lobster emoji, but she'd know that's what I was sending her. She didn't answer though.

Back home after school, scenes were on the chaotic side. Emma was whining about the French lessons she had to go to after school on Mondays. Let's be honest, I'm on her side on this one. Mum has her doing all the ladies' finishing school stuff – French *and* Mandarin, ballet, piano… It's mad. Thank goddess that when I was born my parents were too poor to afford more entertainment for me than a doll's house made out of a cardboard box.

Mum told her the French lessons were non-negotiable and a tantrum threatened to start, so I took Emma to her bedroom for a dance party. She made me listen to Ariana Grande, which I enjoyed more than I let on. After Ariana, she showed me all of her moves to *Shape of You*, singing blithely about how 'my bedsheets smell like you'. Cute cute.

She's actually pretty awesome, my little sister. It took me years to accept that. The changes with Mum and Dad were so abrupt that I couldn't stop myself being angry with her at first. It didn't help that she was an awful baby, always screaming and red, and bald for at least a whole year. I didn't hold her once when she was a baby – I just refused to. But Mum never made a fuss. In fact she was great – she bigged me up so much to Emma over the years that, even though I was horrible to her, Emma always thought I was wonderful. She made me the cutest birthday cards every year, with glitter and hearts and all the works, when Mum and John would get some bog standard piece of paper with *YOU ARE MY MAMA* written in wobbly block letters and nothing more. And so, when I got ready to have her as my little sister, she was right there waiting for me, with her full-body hugs and crazy dance routines and her obsession with ferrets, the worst animal.

She's fun to hang out with, too. She's feisty – always up for an argument. She's creative – good at thinking up reasons why she can't do her homework. She does these spontaneous declarations of love that are the sweetest thing. I don't know where she could have learned that one – not from anyone else in the family, that's for sure!

Lately, though, she's been in a permanent mood. She's been getting into trouble at school with alarming regularity. Mum is forever having to go for meetings with the headteacher and buy forgiveness flowers for the other mothers (oh yes, Emma goes to the sort of school where the dads don't even know what class their child is in). Emma actually got into a sort of fight with another kid the other day, and she also got caught bringing cigarettes to school. Where did she even get cigarettes? Why? I don't think she had any intention of smoking them – just causing trouble. Well, the girl's resourceful, that's for sure. But the worst of it is at home. Emma goes into these rages now, screaming, kicking everything in her path like a tiny pigtailed tornado. The smallest thing can set her off, especially with Mum. She's still the sweetest with me, however, so I just stay out of it when the storm starts brewing.

In the middle of our dancing, my phone beeped. It was Ty, saying sorry he hadn't talked to me in school, and thanking me for doing last night's problem. I wrote back asking how things were with his parents. He said that they seemed worried but were pretending that nothing was going on.

Emma interrupted my anxious thoughts. 'Ooh you're making heart eyes at your phone,' she teased.

'I am not!' I poked her.

She made kissy sounds. 'You're talking to Sa-am, you're talking to Sa-am,' she sing-sang.

My stomach flip-flopped on itself. Had I really been making eyes at my phone? Is that how I look when I'm talking to Ty? I need to snap out of it. I mean sure, I can't help that I heavily enjoy the gift of Ty's appearance, but I can't start making things awkward if I'm going to be spending lots of time with him. Not to mention that it's not fair on Sam.

Sam! I suddenly remembered that he'd sent me his application, but I hadn't had time to look at it. I promised myself I'd do it soon.

I put my phone away in my room and the two of us went downstairs for dinner, which was a very delicious homemade quiche. Mum hadn't made anything that elaborate for years. I squinted at her suspiciously. She was looking a bit flushed, and young, and pretty. If I wasn't careful, people would start saying stuff like *that can't be your mother, you two look like sisters!*

'Why are you looking so good?'

'Don't I always look good?' she challenged.

'Yeah, but... wait – you got a hair trim!' I suddenly realised.

'Yes, I did,' Mum said, turning distinctly pink. 'That's allowed, isn't it? I went for a walk at lunch, saw a hair salon and thought why not?'

'It looks really nice,' I said. Which it did, only there is the fact that Mum religiously gets her hair trimmed every two months exactly, always at the same place.

'Thank you,' she beamed.

After the quiche we had the leftovers of yesterday's cake, except for John who isn't 'into desserts'. The conversation was not especially pleasant and I'll admit a fair share of responsibility for this. First, John told us that he'd be even less around than usual in the coming days. I didn't exactly react to this news with tears, but Emma looked quietly upset. Apparently, there's been some sort of disaster at the bank where John works.

'Oh, are all the billionaires scared of losing their money?' I said. I was probably smirking a bit – I couldn't help myself.

John looked stressed and changed the subject, so then we argued about a petition that's circulating to get the voting age lowered to sixteen.

John: Really? You think sixteen-year-olds are mature enough to vote?

Me: Well, if sixteen-year-olds could vote, there would have been no Brexit.

John: Okay—

Me: So maybe instead, we should stop people voting *after* a certain age.

John: Fair point, Clara, fair point.

Yeah, John backs down easily.

I glanced at Mum, who normally makes nasty faces at me if I'm mean to John. She didn't even seem to be listening – she was mindlessly scooping frosting off her slice of cake with her finger and licking it, a faint smile on her lips.

Tuesday 11th October

Ty told me today before Maths class started that he'd heard his parents discussing Oli. 'Dad said, "Do you think he's done it again?"'

'Done what?' I asked.

'I don't know,' Ty said, frustrated. 'Oli's done plenty of stuff that he's got into trouble for but nothing... nothing that would cause him to *disappear*. So I've been thinking it over, and there's only one thing I remember that might have something to do with this.' He paused. 'About five years ago, Oli went away for a while. Mum and Dad told me he was doing a computing course in Hong Kong and I just accepted it at the time because I had no reason not to. But thinking back to it now, of course he wasn't in Hong Kong. He's never talked about the trip since – you'd think that an experience like that when you're fifteen would have made some sort of impression. And I remember that when he came home from the trip, he gave me a crappy tourist key-ring as a souvenir. Even back then I thought that was strange – Oli never normally brought me anything back from his trips. I guess my parents made him do it because they really wanted me to believe the story.'

'So what do you think he was doing instead?'

Ty just shrugged.

'Well, he came back that time,' I pointed out. 'And he seemed normal. So if the same thing is happening again, whatever it is – that's a good sign, isn't it?'

'Yeah,' Ty agreed. 'He did come back. But it's not exactly the same... he wrote to me that time. Only once in the whole month, which was way less often than usual. But still, he wrote. Not like now.'

'He did leave you that note,' I said. 'And it's been way less than a month.'

Ty's shoulders seemed to relax a bit at that. 'Yes, you're right.' He sighed. 'I wish my parents would just tell me what they know, but they're still pretending everything is fine around me.'

Mr Howard walked in then, and Ty turned around. I could see his jaw clicking nervously. What had Oli done five years go? He was already working then, Ty had said. He was already making money from hacking companies' security systems. Had he got in trouble? Hacked someone he shouldn't have? I wondered what Ty was imagining in his own crazy scenarios.

M wasn't in school again today, and when I checked my phone at lunch she still hadn't answered yesterday's message. I sent her another one and put my phone away, disconcerted. I shuffled to Further Maths and slumped into the seat next to Xavier.

Xavier: Wild night?

Me: You can't even imagine.

Xavier: [raising one eyebrow in the way that I can't do] Oh yeah I can.

Me: Stop that! Actually, I was just up late doing homework.

Xavier: Same here. The teachers have all gone mad!

Me: Yeah, they really have.

Xavier: Look at who actually had a wild night though [he cocked his chin towards Natasha, who was fast asleep, her head balanced perfectly on her hand, her soft cult-member-length hair draped around her shoulders. She sat next to an empty seat, as always.]

Me: Maybe she just did extra homework too.

Xavier: No way, she was doing vodka shots with all her gorgeous spy friends that don't go to our school.

Natasha let out a tiny, musical snore, looking mysterious as ever.

Me: You know what? That sounds more likely.

Xavier: Alice has got some wild theories about Natasha – thinks she's exiled royalty.

Me: Alice? You talked about Natasha with Alice?

Xavier: Yeah, Alice loves making up people's backstories.

Me: I didn't know the two of you were friends!

Xavier: Of course, I've known her for ages.

Me: Through Ty?

Xavier: No, from way before. I only became friends with Ty after the two of them got together. Actually, when Alice and I first met Ty we both thought he fancied us. She was right, unfortunately for me [he made a disappointed face].

I was completely amazed. I had no idea Alice and Xavier had known each other for a long time. I'd never noticed them talking to each other at school. And the way he talked about her. She sounded fun – like someone I'd want to be friends with. M and I spend ages making up random people's backstories.

So, Xavier was friends with both Ty and Alice. I was too curious – I couldn't help myself.

Me: So... Alice and Ty—

Mr Howard: Ms Valentine! No matter who you're sitting next to, it's just nonstop chatting with you!

Me: I'm sorry, I'll stop!

Mr Howard: Come be sorry over here where I can see you [he pointed to a desk in front of him.]

Me: Oh no, please, I'll be quiet I promise.

Mr Howard: I don't think you even know what quiet means.

I grumbled to Xavier as I gathered my stuff – he just giggled, very happy to be the lucky one. 'I'll miss you,' he mouthed as he waved me goodbye.

I couldn't concentrate for the rest of the lesson, too frustrated that I hadn't had a chance to ask about Alice and Ty. When would I get another opportunity like that? Never, that's when.

School finished at 4pm. I suddenly realised that this was the time Dad had said on the phone to the mysterious 'Rachie'. Was Mum arriving at his restaurant right now? We used to go all the time when Dad first opened it. We wrote the opening menu all together. My pick was eggs and soldiers (I was six years old, remember!) Dad put it on the breakfast menu and made them the best soldiers ever, with lots of dripping butter. He said people ordered them all the time and I felt so proud.

Mum's pick was spaghetti all'Amatriciana. There's a cute story behind that dish – Dad made it for a famous old Italian chef once and the guy scribbled a note to the effect that he was officially accepted as honorary countryman. Dad has the note framed in his office at the restaurant. The dish hasn't been on the menu for years now, but old customers still request it and Dad will usually indulge them.

The restaurant is really, really nice. It's the sort of place that everyone likes, young people, old people, families, couples on dates, birthday diners. There are lots of regulars who know everyone's name and eat there at least once a week. Everyone has a favourite dish and they always have a mini riot when Dad takes it off the menu. He likes the riots, they make him feel special. It's basically exactly the place he talked about opening all those years he was working at the River Café.

At 4pm, the restaurant wouldn't be very busy but it would still be bustling. There'd be people writing great works on their laptops or having the late coffee they know will keep them up at night. (That's what they say when they order, every time: 'I shouldn't be ordering this now, I'll be up all night' and then you ask, 'Do you want decaf, then?' and they make a face like that's the most offensive thing they've ever heard.) At that time of day, it's mostly people who don't have an office and are getting a bit of work done outside of their home, and they are always in the mood to have long conversations with you if you make the mistake of lingering too long near their table.

I know all this because I sometimes waitress there during the holidays for a bit of money. It's a good workout too – there's a flight of stairs down to the kitchen when we have to bring down super-heavy containers of dirty dishes and then bring back up even-heavier containers of clean glasses and cutlery. And since I'm the boss' daughter I never get put on toilet-mopping duty, I always get great meals from the kitchen, and Jess (the restaurant manager and, as Dad likes to tell me, the second most important person in his life) never puts me on the morning shift. Yay, nepotism!

It's really a fun place to work, and the people-watching is good. I've had some great outfit ideas working there. In fact, I've only ever had one bad experience, when Alice showed up with her parents for dinner. We exchanged horrified looks and silently agreed to act as if we had never met. Of course, they were sat in my section and I had to be very polite, call her 'miss' even if it made me choke, and write down all her food substitutions with a smile. Makes me shudder just thinking about it. Who orders fish and chips with the batter taken off the fish?!

I was almost tempted to go over to the restaurant right then to see if I could catch Mum and Dad together. I smiled to myself. M would totally have done it – she'd have dressed up in disguise to spy on them and everything.

Thinking of M made me worried again. I looked at my phone, but still nothing. It's not like her at all, she never does the not-replying thing. If she's angry at me, she normally texts in ALL CAPS relentlessly. I can't help getting this all-over frosty feeling I recognise from a period a few years ago, when Amanda wasn't well.

Back then, M would sometimes stop answering me for a day or two, or not show up for our plans, and then later the phone would ring and she'd have such a tiny, fragile voice. I will never ever forget the way she sounded through the phone on those calls. Mum and I would stop whatever we were doing, drive over and help her to convince Amanda to come to the mental-health clinic where they knew her. We never knew how we'd find Amanda when we went there. Sometimes she was in the best of moods, naked and dancing around the house, having taken M out of school because she had an urge to go to a fair and ride on the Ferris wheel and eat cotton candy. Other times she might be in tears, convinced she had diabetes and couldn't find her syringes anywhere.

I knew that this happened a lot more often than what we saw, that M only called us when she couldn't fix things on her own. She never wanted to talk about it when we came, just trailed along behind us silently with sea-filled eyes as we coaxed Amanda into getting in Mum's car. M, who can talk about literally anything else. Eventually, Amanda started taking medication. It took a while for them to find something that worked right, but now she's been doing great for years. I'd almost forgotten about all of it, until now.

I'd worked myself up so much that I decided I would just tell M everything if she asked me any questions: about Ty, Oli, everything. But when I called her, the conversation didn't go at all as I expected. She picked up on the very first ring.

'Hi...'

'M! How are you feeling?'

'Oh!' She made a fake sounding cough. '*Cough cough...* A bit better.'

'Is Amanda ok?'

'What? Yes, she's fine.'

I relaxed a bit. M sounded quiet, but she didn't have the shaky voice I remembered from years ago. 'Shall I come see you now? I don't have any plans,' I said.

'No, no, you don't want to catch anything.'

I hesitated. This was also extremely unlike M. She thinks germs are healthy for you and will happily eat crisps off the floor of the Tube if she drops some when she is drunk (often). And she is not good about being cooped up at home. A little cough would never stop her from asking me to come and distract her. But when I tried again, she insisted I shouldn't come. I figured that at least this way I would be able to go home, hole up in my bedroom and learn all I could about RSA encryption, which I hadn't had the time to do at all yet.

'Ok,' I said finally, when she refused to change her mind. 'I hope you feel better soon. I missed you a lot in school today.'

'I missed you too,' she said softly.

At home, I settled on my bed with Singh's book. I read the table of contents again, but there was no mention of RSA encryption. I flipped a few pages and got engrossed despite myself in a chapter about Mary Queen of Scots, when suddenly something went *ding* in my head. I flipped back to the table of contents, and there it was: a chapter called *The Birth of Public Key Cryptography*. Public key – those were the words from Oli's question, which I had copied carefully at the top of a blank page in my notebook:

Question 266: Decode the RSA-encoded message 90 encrypted with the public key (247,11).

I flipped to the chapter near the end of the book and sure enough, there was a whole section on RSA encryption. I learned that the RSA coding system is built around prime numbers, which are for sure my favourite mathematical object. I think it's so crazy that something can have such a simple definition but be so difficult to study.

A prime number is a whole number (apart from the number 1) that can't be divided by anything apart from 1 and itself. We learned about them in primary school and I asked Emma about them once and she could recite lots of them: 2, 3, 5, 7, 11, 13, 17, 19, 23, 29...

They are the building blocks of every other number: every number is made up of prime numbers multiplied together. For example, 15 is 3x5, 49 is 7x7, 42 is 2x3x7, 180 is 2x2x3x3x3x5.

Once you've figured out which prime numbers make up your number when multiplied together, you say that you've found its prime factors. So, another way of describing a prime number is by saying that prime numbers are the numbers whose only prime factor is themselves.

With such a simple definition, it feels like they should be the easiest thing to understand, but actually, mathematicians have barely been able to prove anything about them at all. They don't seem to follow any sort of pattern or obey any general rules. And even with the rules that mathematicians are pretty sure they *do* follow, lots of them have not been proven. (Actually there's a rich guy that will give you a million dollars if you prove some of them! It's on my list of life goals, I'll let you know how I get on.) Pretty much the only thing we know about prime numbers is that there is an infinite number of them, and that's something that has been known since Euclid – so it's not much to show for over two thousand years of maths.

The main thing we've done since Euclid is to find more prime numbers, especially since computers have been invented. We're up to testing numbers that are so large nowadays that it takes computers years and years to figure out if they are prime. (It's so weird to imagine a computer taking years to do something. The little loading sign on someone's Instagram story can *feel* like years, but this is actual, literal years!) Every time a new prime number gets discovered, people get really excited (ok, mathematicians get excited, normal people maybe less so) and that's even though we *know* that there are infinitely many. It's because prime numbers are so unpredictable that each one is exciting. They're like the four-leaf clovers of numbers.

Anyway – that's what the RSA encryption system depends on: the fact that when given a very large number, it's actually very hard to factorise it into its prime factors. The principle of the RSA code is that you can give everyone (even your enemies) your public key, which contains two numbers. The first of those is a very large number that you've obtained by multiplying together two big prime numbers. You keep the two prime numbers secret, but you can make their product public – if your number is big enough, your enemies won't be able to find its prime factors for years using their computers.

Since you make your key public, that means that anyone can *encrypt* using it, but it isn't possible to *decrypt* any messages if you don't know the two prime numbers you keep secret. This means that anyone can write a message using your code, they just won't be able to decode what other people's messages mean. The only thing that can go wrong is if someone manages to factorise your large number and find your two primes – then you are in a lot of trouble.

Of course, Oli hadn't actually given us an impossibly large number to factorise in his public key, otherwise his code would have been, well, impossible to break – instead, he'd given us 247. I divided it by every prime number in turn, starting with 2, 3, 5, 7, 11 etc, and pretty soon I found 247=13x19. So now, I had the two secret primes that allow you to decode messages (obviously this is the bit you couldn't do if this was a real code used to send messages during a war).

After that, I just had to follow the steps that were described in the book, using the second number from the public key that Oli had given us, and pretty soon I had the answer.

I grabbed my phone, excited to tell Ty. The screen flashed at me – it was almost 9pm, and I realised I was starving. I went downstairs. Mum hadn't come home. It was getting so late that John panicked and tried to make us food. He managed to both over-boil and undercook the pasta, which I was not aware was even possible. The spaghetti strands were stuck together in big clumps, mushy on the outside and still crunchy in the middle. He stared at his creation silently for a minute or so, then ordered in Chinese food. 'Good idea,' I told him. 'Know your limits.' He made half a smile.

Mum eventually showed up as we were watching TV, looking unconcerned. John had acted with us like her absence was totally expected, but it wasn't very good acting.

'We've got leftovers,' I said.

'Oh, I already ate,' Mum said breezily.

'What did you eat?' Emma piped up. 'I had all of the sweet-and-sour pork for myself because Clara doesn't like it. Daddy tried to make spaghetti,' Emma shook her head.

'I see,' Mum said, stroking her hair. 'Well, I had spaghetti myself, actually. With tomato sauce and bacon. Spaghetti all'Amatriciana.'

Wednesday 12th October

I dreamt that M was floating out in the middle of a huge pool and one by one her limbs started floating away from her. I jumped in to try to help her but no matter how hard I swam I didn't get any closer.

I woke up in a panic, heart racing, and ran to school. She wasn't there again, and she hadn't messaged to tell me. I stared forlornly at her empty seat. At least, since I wasn't chatting to anyone, Mr Howard didn't even look in my direction once.

If you're reading this for the Oli updates, you're in luck – we got somewhere today, finally. Ty didn't have football practice so we agreed that we'd walk together to his after school. At the end of the day, I came out with the rush of people. Ty was already there, holding his skateboard against his leg. I tried to stop myself, but I couldn't help feeling excited that it was me he was waiting for. When he saw me, his eyes lit up for a totally perfect second. He took the skateboard under his arm and we set off towards his.

'You're amazing,' he said, making my neck tingly, 'doing the questions so quickly.'

'I'm finding it easier and easier to learn stuff on my own, actually,' I told him. 'I'm starting to understand how to go about thinking things through myself without someone to guide me.'

Ty laughed. 'I guess that's what Oli was hoping I would do.'

'Well, I'm finding it really interesting. Maybe I'll have to keep the computer after this is – over...' My voice faded as I finished the sentence. I wasn't sure if Ty would be upset that I'd just been all excited about the maths problems. Obviously, this whole thing was so much more serious than that. But when I glanced at him, he seemed preoccupied with something else. 'Is something wrong?' I asked.

'I don't really know,' he said. 'There's been a new development. Yesterday, two guys from GCHQ came over. The security and intelligence organisation.'

'What! Oh my god, were they looking for Oli?' I asked.

'They were... but when I asked them why, they wouldn't give me any details. They just asked if Oli had said anything to me about where he was going or what he was doing, or if he had left anything for me before leaving.' Ty shrugged.

'Did you tell them about the note?'

'I didn't,' he said. 'If he's in trouble for something, I don't want to be getting him deeper into it. One of them gave me his card, look.'

He took a card out of his wallet and handed it to me. The name listed was Stuart Ashby, and his department was the National Cyber Security Centre.

I looked up at Ty. 'Cyber security,' I read out loud.

'Yeah.' Ty winced. 'What on earth is Oli up to?' He sighed and put the card back in his wallet. 'They told me to give the card to my parents and have them call, but I didn't do that either. I figure that if it's serious, GCHQ will come back anyway, and maybe we can get into Oli's computer before then.' He looked worried, but then he shook the feeling away and smiled at me. 'I'm sure we'll find stuff out pretty soon. I have a feeling this is the last question.'

'Well, if you have a *feeling*, it must be,' I said.

He laughed, and I saw him relax a bit. I didn't know what to think about what he'd just told me. It might not mean anything, of course – GCHQ could be interested in Oli for any number of reasons. Maybe someone he knew had committed a crime, not him. Maybe they even just wanted to recruit him or needed his expertise on something. It might be nothing. But on the other hand, be it might not be nothing at all... I tried to recall if I'd seen anything about cyber crime in the news, but there were no stories that I could remember.

We got to Ty's place. In the bedroom, his sheets had been changed, to another blue set, a darker blue. He had hidden the computer under his mattress, which he lifted with one arm to slide the laptop out. He turned it on, I typed in my answer and felt my heart sink. I'd pressed the enter button, but nothing had happened. The screen stayed unchanged, with no black tick.

I felt myself breathing really fast. I thought I must have got the answer wrong or even broken the computer. Then, some extra words popped up on the screen: *Message in letters, not numbers,* the words said.

I turned to Ty. 'I don't understand – how could it be in letters? The code only gives numbers, I promise!' I showed him the page in my notebook with the calculations, and the answer at the bottom: 181.

Ty didn't say anything but he started mouthing silent words and counting on his fingers, and then a little smile spread to the corners of his mouth. 'The message is AHA,' he said. 'It's just counting the position of the letters in the alphabet, you know: A is 1, B is 2 etc. Oli always said that I needed to experience a real *AHA moment,* when everything clicks into place. He said if I had it even just one time, I'd get hooked on it like him. Hasn't happened yet, though.'

'Well, this was like a mini AHA moment,' I smiled.

'Yeah, for a pre-schooler maybe. I know the alphabet and can count on my fingers, incredible!'

'Here, you type it in.' I turned the laptop towards him.

He typed carefully, his long index finger pressing down each key with a click. The A key from the computer stuck a bit and Ty had to press down extra hard for it to work. But then, as soon as he had pressed *enter*, I knew that he'd been right and this time was it – we'd done the final question. The screen blinked a couple of times, and with our hearts thumping, we both waited for the desktop screen to come up as the computer whirred lightly.

'What were you saying about my *feeling*, then?' Ty said to me, clearly excited.

'I apologise,' I smiled. 'I will never discount your feelings again.'

Whoops, there were too many possible meanings to this one. I swear he stared at me for a moment too long.

When the desktop appeared, the background image was a picture of Ty. He must have been about ten, but he looked pretty much the same as he does now, just with a bowl haircut that covered his eyes and a sort of impish grin that I've never seen on his older face. He was standing in the middle of a room wrapped up in a huge towel and laughing at the camera. Next to him, an older boy was about to grab the towel and pull it off, looking very pleased with himself. I glanced sideways at Ty. He was smiling at the screen. He'd also gone a bit red.

I turned my attention back to the screen. The computer seemed very empty. I'm not an expert – I wouldn't know how to find hidden stuff on a computer or anything, but from a quick look around it was very bare. There were just a few icons on the sidebar (Google Chrome, Photoshop, the bin, Skype, that kind of thing) one folder on the desktop called just *documents*, and nothing else. We opened the folder and found a couple of scans of bills. There definitely wasn't anything personal, and not even any work.

'There's nothing here,' Ty said, deflated. 'This is crazy – I've seen Oli use this computer before and it didn't look like this at all. It had all sorts of things in it. It sort of... synced up with his other computer.' He frowned, not saying the obvious: Oli must have stopped the sync and cleared everything before leaving.

Ty clicked around aimlessly, discouraged by this anticlimactic reveal after all our efforts. I didn't know what to say so, well, I said nothing. Then Ty seemed to have an idea, and he brought up the Chrome browser and went to gmail. We both held our breath as the page loaded. I squeezed my eyes shut, and when I reopened them, Ty was gripping my arm, and we were inside Oli's inbox.

Only, it didn't look right. None of the emails had been read for the last few days.

'He hasn't looked at any of these,' Ty said. 'When's the last email he read?'

He scrolled down. At some point on the 5th the emails went from mostly read and answered, to all unread. Just before that point, I could see an email from Ty asking Oli to please answer his calls – Oli had read it but hadn't written back. Around the same time, however, Oli had answered an email from someone called Karim. Ty clicked on it, but it was a work question that was pretty much gibberish to me.

Most of the unanswered emails from before the 5th were from a girl called Cécile, who seemed very angry judging by the all caps, exclamation-mark-heavy subjects. Aside from Cécile and that one email from Ty, Oli had a very high answer rate.

'Is Cécile the girl you went to see?' I asked.

'No,' Ty said. 'I have no idea who this Cécile is. Guess there's plenty of stuff Oli doesn't tell me.' He looked a bit dejected. He clicked on one of Cécile's latest. 'It looks like he broke up with her two months ago and she's still pretty upset with him.

He hasn't been answering her – she's not too happy about that either.' The message Ty had just clicked on read, *You fucker, can't even be bothered to answer my emails now?* and then, *I JUST WANT TO COME AND GET MY FAVOURITE SHIRT THAT BELONGED TO MY GRANDMA WHO IS NOW DEAD, ASSHOLE!!!* Well, let's be honest – she had a point.

Ty scrolled back up to where the emails were all unread. There were a couple of marketing emails, and lots of work ones, including one more from Karim. Ty clicked on that one. Karim had actually written twice in a row. A few days ago he'd written, *Where r u man?* And yesterday, he'd followed up with a message that said, *Tried tracking your phone and not getting any joy. Either you've got way better than me or you're dead, haha. No, but I'm getting worried now, u ok?*

Ty clicked on another work email, but that one was just about having found where the error was in some code. Ty went back to the inbox and clicked on another one: *Dear Mr. Rai, I hope this finds you well. We were expecting your report on Friday – please update us on its status. With my best wishes.*

'No one knows where he is,' Ty said slowly.

He marked the emails we'd looked at as unread again and scrolled down the page, back to the ones from the 6th. We could see little bits of Oli's replies for each one he'd responded to, and I started to recognise the names that came back often, the personal emails with no caps in the subject, the professional ones titled: *Checking in* or *Confirming receipt of invoice.*

Then suddenly an email caught my eye, one Oli hadn't replied to, in the middle of others he had. The sender came up only as *SPAM*. The subject was one word: *Meeting.* 'That one!' I exclaimed in a low breath (I wonder why you start whispering when something exciting happens), but Ty had already noticed and clicked on it.

Dear Oliver,

We would like to invite you to join us to-morrow. If you accept, a car will pick you up at an agreed time and location.

With our best wishes,

SPAM

Underneath, like it was their logo, there was a spiral design. The email was from the 4th.

Ty looked at me. 'That's the day Oli left,' he said.

'Do you think he took up their invitation?'

'I have no idea. He never mentioned this to me. And he never answered that email.'

He copied the sender's email address and searched for more messages sent by the same person, but it was the only one. There was nothing either in the bin or the – Ty managed a giggle at this – spam folder. 'There's no way of knowing if he went to that meeting or not'.

'Who are these people – why would someone call themselves *spam*?' I mused.

'I know, it's so weird. It seems a sure-fire way to make sure the person you're writing to doesn't read it.'

'Maybe it's someone's idea of a joke to call their company that?'

Ty went on Google and searched for *spam*. Obviously, the only things that came up were ham, and unwanted emails and how to avoid them. We googled *Spam company* and *Spam company name* but nothing came up. *Spam spiral*, *Spam maths* and *Spam Oliver Rai* also didn't give any results (though I did learn that Oli's middle name is Manesh and also a picture of him came up. It was a bit like if Ty stopped sports, took up smiling ironically, and melted his face with the boy from *Stranger Things*.)

Ty went more and more silent as we searched and didn't find anything. Soon, I was the only one suggesting more things to look up. The excitement from getting into Oli's email was evaporating.

Suddenly the page reloaded on its own, and we were locked out of Oli's email. A message appeared, telling us that someone had logged into the inbox on another device. Ty and I looked at each other.

'Oli's looking at his emails right now!' Ty exclaimed. He looked at his phone, obviously hoping for a message to appear there.

'Do you think he could tell someone else was looking at the same time?'

'Are you saying he's locked us out on purpose?'

'I don't know,' I said. 'It could also have happened automatically – maybe he set it up so that you can't be logged in on two devices at once. Try refreshing the page,' I suggested.

When Ty did, the page didn't seem to have locked us out permanently, but it was asking us to log in again. The box for Oli's password was already filled in in neat little black dots. Ty glanced at me and clicked *enter*, but the pop-up didn't go away – instead, there was some new text: *Unexpected activity. Please answer your secret question to continue, or request a code be sent to your saved number: XXXXXXXX112*

'That's Oli's number,' Ty said moodily, 'so it's not an option.'

I clicked to view the secret question.

> **Secret question:** Are there more rational or irrational numbers?

Ty covered his face with his hands.

'Are you crying or laughing?' I asked.

'I don't know,' he said from behind his hands. 'Both?'

'Well... I don't know what rational and irrational numbers are,' I said. 'But I'll figure it out.'

'I know,' he said quietly. He let his hands drop from his face and looked at me. 'I know you will.'

'At least it doesn't seem like we're locked out for good,' I said to make him feel better.

'You're right,' Ty said stoically. 'You'll find the answer, we'll get back in, and we'll be able to see any messages that Oli is writing... like, right now.' He glanced at his phone again.

'Hey Ty...' I opened my mouth, already regretting what I was about to say. 'Are you sure you don't want to tell your parents anything? Maybe they should know. I mean, the fact that Oli hadn't looked at his emails in all this time, even for work... and the note he left you. Maybe they'd understand what it all means.'

Huh – I really did just say that, I thought. Well, I guess my brain was doing the sensible thing, but my heart was screaming *Stop talking! I get to spend all this time with Ty and you're going to ruin it!*

Ty was on my heart's side though. 'I can't do that,' he said. 'Oli'd kill me. The note literally says one thing – don't tell Mum and Dad. He even says *please.*' He shook his head. 'Oli never says please. No, he's probably just out somewhere working on some project, whatever it is, and he'll come back looking all innocent soon, asking what all the fuss is about. He doesn't like outside distractions when he's working...' He made an attempt at a smile. 'Honestly, sometimes I think Oli isn't even working on anything at all, and this is all one big ploy to make me finally give the maths questions a real go.'

'Ok,' I said.

'Let's just give it a bit longer.'

'Ok,' I repeated.

I could see him hesitating, torn between doing what Oli had asked in his note, and the fact that what we'd found on Oli's computer was definitely not normal.

'Half-term,' he said finally. 'If we haven't figured it out by then, I'll tell my parents.' He nodded to himself.

Suddenly his phone rang, interrupting his thoughts, and I saw Alice's perfect face fill the screen. Ty pressed the ignore button.

'That was Alice?'

He nodded.

'Have you told her? About the computer?'

He didn't answer for a few seconds, just pinched his lips together and looked towards the ceiling but then he said, 'I haven't told her anything about this. Actually... we broke up yesterday.'

I held myself stock still, like if I never moved again then time wouldn't move either from this moment. I searched around for the perfect thing to say. And what do you think my brain found? The following gem: 'I have a boyfriend.'

I have a boyfriend. Seriously?!! I mean, good on my brain for keeping me at religious-zealot levels of good behaviour, but really? Could it not let me enjoy this moment and cope with just a few more minutes of moral greyness? Pious brain went on, undaunted. 'He's called Sam. We've been together for three years.'

Ty was looking a bit surprised by this point. 'I don't think I've ever met him', he said in a tentative voice.

'Yeah, I know. He goes to another school. We just see each other at home and stuff.'

'Ok.'

For the first time, there was an awkward silence between us. We eased back into it after a moment, but the moment never quite passed. The whole time, I could feel it hanging in the space between us, full of muddled thoughts that I didn't know how to iron out. I left not long after.

I'm home now. It was eerily quiet when I came in – the kind of quiet that you just know in your bones is the result of a calamitous event. Anyway, it turns out that Emma has been suspended until the end of the week. She *bit* a girl! Like, with her teeth! And then she said a very bad swear word beginning with a c, which it seems was brand new vocabulary for around 80% of her class. So now, 100% of the parents are very, very angry at Mum.

Mum was sitting at the kitchen table in the dark like a ghost, drinking a glass of her special Georgian skin-contact wine like it was one of the £5 bottles we bring to parties. I turned on the lights and she looked at me like a bruised owl, blinking very fast. She told me the story in an exhausted monotone, drank up the rest of her glass and got up. 'Can you deal with your sister tonight?' she asked. 'I need a break.'

I climbed up the stairs. Emma was asleep on top of her covers, fully clothed, having passed out from all her hard work at creating disasters. She was flushed pink and angelic-looking. I shook her gently so she would wake up and change into her pyjamas, but she batted my hand away in her sleep so I left her to it.

| 4 |

The Hilbert Hotel Paradox

Thursday 13th October

Home from school today. There was a crisis this morning when my angel sister's babysitter abruptly quit after ten minutes on the job, citing unreasonable behaviour and demanding compensation for psychological damages. I was the only person free to look after the sweet princess who, you'll recall, is suspended. (If, of course, by *free*, you mean willing to give up a day of precious education.)

In any case, the dear child has been pretty easy to wrangle, and you'll be happy to learn that I have made her into a detective sidekick, and together we had a major breakthrough. But that didn't happen until the afternoon. First, she spent the morning sulking in her room, not needing any attention from me. A bit after noon I made lunch for the two of us and showed her a maths problem to get her mind off her weighty troubles. I find it quite fun doing stuff like that with Emma, seeing her understand things because of how I explain them to her and watching her work stuff out on her own. It always makes me think that maybe I would like to be a teacher, only then I remember my disastrous tutoring experiences with other kids who don't get things as quickly as she does. Turns out I don't exactly have patience.

Mr Howard talked to us recently in class about the concept of infinity. He said that by having the little ∞ symbol and a name for it, we make it easy to discuss things. For example, we can write, nice and short: $1/\infty = 0$. But we need to remember that this sort of language is actually a shortcut. Infinity isn't a number, and it doesn't really fit into equations like a number does. It's a concept that's very hard for us to really grasp because we don't have any actual example of it in the world. Even, for example, the number of grains of sand on Earth, is just a number. A really huge one, ok, but still just a number, which makes it very different from actual infinity. When you start to explore what happens in an infinite world, you realise just how different it is to our world of big numbers.

I told Emma about the Hilbert Hotel paradox. 'Imagine,' I said, 'that you've got the most incredible, fancy hotel, which has an infinite number of rooms. The rooms are numbered, as in all hotels. The numbers go in order: 1, 2, 3 and so on, forever, since your hotel is infinite. It's such an amazing hotel that it is completely full. You have an infinite number of guests staying in all your rooms, making you very rich and happy. But suddenly, a new guest arrives in the lobby and asks for a room. Because you are a great saleswoman, you tell them that of course, a room will be ready in just ten minutes! How can you make good on your promise?' I asked.

Emma looked totally bemused. 'But that's impossible, all the rooms are full!'

I helped her a bit. 'Yes, it would be impossible in the normal world,' I agreed, 'but remember that you're in infinite world right now. I'll give you a hint. You tell your new guest that they can go to Room 1. Of course, then you will have to move the guest that was already in Room 1. Where can you put that person?'

Emma scrunched up her little button nose, 'All the other rooms are full, so if I tell them to go to a room, they'll have to make the person there move as well...'

'That's right!' I said, 'so what if you tell the person who was in Room 1 to go to Room 2, and then—'

She interrupted suddenly, a spark of understanding lighting up in her eyes. 'I know! I can move the guest that was in Room 2 and put them in Room 3, and then move the guest in Room 3 to Room 4, and I can do that with all the guests – just move them up one room, and it will work because we can go all the way up to infinity!' She looked very pleased with herself.

'That's exactly it,' I agreed. 'You get on your fancy announcement system and you say to everyone, ok, pack your bags and please move to the room which is one number up from the one you are currently in. It won't take more than ten minutes (unless some of the guests are very slow packers like you), and your new guest will get their room.'

'They need to change the sheets though.'

'That's true,' I agreed. 'Maybe ten minutes was a little ambitious. You got ahead of yourself there.'

She smiled.

'Are you ready for a harder one?' I asked.

Emma nodded excitedly.

'Right, so your hotel is full again, but now a whole bus full of people arrives. It has 100 people in it, and again, in full saleswoman mode, you tell them that you will have a room ready for each of them in just... one hour. What do you do?'

Emma looked at me with mild contempt. 'That one's not any harder, I can just do the same trick as before! I get my megaphone and tell everyone to move to the room that is 100 more than their current one – and that makes rooms 1, 2, 3... up to 100 free for the new guests.'

'Ok smartypants,' I said, 'here's a *really* hard one for you then. Your hotel is still full, and a new bus full of people arrives. Only this time it's an *infinite* bus, with an *infinite* number of people, and they all want a room! Before you can stop yourself, you tell them that it's no problem, they can all get rooms in an hour. Quick, what are you going to do this time?'

Emma frowned and put her head in her hands. She suddenly looked about ten years older, almost an adult – muttering to herself exactly like I do when I've got a hard problem to solve. 'I can't use the same trick as before – I can't tell people to move to infinity more than their current number!' She said under her breath. Then suddenly I remembered why I do not in fact want to become a teacher because Emma gave me a black look and wailed, 'Your stupid problem is *too hard!*'

The ten extra years dropped off her and about six more. Now she looked more like she used to when she was two years old, trying stubbornly to convince her triangle shape to fit into the round hole.

'No one in my class got this one either, I was just checking to see how much of a genius you are,' I said. 'Turns out just a little bit genius, not a major genius. What a disappointment.'

She laughed, the tantrum evaporating.

'Ok, take your megaphone,' I said, and gave her a rolled-up piece of paper. 'Now tell everyone, "Please pack up all your things and move to the room whose number is double your current one."'

'Everyone move to the room whose number is double your current number!' Emma shouted diligently.

'Can you see what will happen?'

She thought for a while.

'Where will the guest from Room 1 go to?' I prompted.

'Room 2,' she said, unimpressed that I was quizzing her on her 2-times tables.

'And the guest who was in Room 2?' I asked again.

'They go to Room 4,' she said. 'And the guest who was in Room 3 goes to Room 6 – oh!' she exclaimed, wide-eyed. 'All the guests will have moved to even-numbered rooms: 2, 4, 6, 8, etc. But all the odd numbers will now be free: 1, 3, 5, 7 – all of those. And there's an infinite number of them, enough for all my new guests!' She gave me her imp smile. 'That was pretty cool. I think I like the infinite world.'

After this success I went to pick up my phone which had been charging by my bed all day. There were a few messages asking where I was, a video of a puppy kissing a duck from Sam, Friday's cinema showings with a question mark, also from

Sam, and nothing from M. And one message from Ty – a blurry photo of my empty seat with a question mark.

Family emergency, I texted.

All ok?? he fired back immediately.

I shook my head – how could I have forgotten that family emergency meant something quite different in his world right now. *Yes, totally fine, my baby sister is just acting up and I was the only available babysitter.*

You have a sister? You really are full of surprises.

I paused. Was he referring to having just learned about Sam? My heartbeat got noticeably quicker in my chest.

As I was pondering what to answer, he started typing again. It seemed to go on for ages, and then: *Can you come over later?*

I don't think I'll have finished the question, I told him.

It's not about that. I want to talk to you about something.

My thumbs hovered over the screen. Not about the question? *Ok*, I typed, and hit send with my heart all the way in my throat.

I had been working hard at avoiding thinking about last night's conversation (this involved impressive feats of mental distraction. A sort of Tibetan-monk-level meditation, really). *Alice and Ty's stuff has nothing to do with me,* I told myself sternly. But now Ty was making it very hard indeed. Could I be wrong? It seemed impossible that I would be able to wait several hours to *talk about something,* as he said. I was pretty sure the clock had started ticking at half-speed as well.

I was a touch euphemistic in my message to Ty, given that I haven't even started thinking about Oli's secret question yet. I had so much homework that had been piling up since I'd been spending so much time on Oli's questions that I got in trouble with two different teachers for not having done something this week. On top of that, Mr Kelly had finally read my personal statement for uni applications, and apparently I use too many filler words. He deleted about 30% of my draft and would not accept my complaint that he was cramping my literary style, so I have to redo it for him to check again.

I felt too antsy about Ty's message to think about maths, so instead I decided to see if I could figure out who SPAM was. I just couldn't think of anything apart from penis-enlargement ads and gross sandwich fillings.

Spam Spam Spam.

I lay down on my bed and stared at the ceiling, begging for an idea. Then I realised something: it wasn't *spam*, it was *SPAM*, in capital letters! Could it be an acronym? I started trying to imagine what it could stand for. S for... society? Googling *SPAM Society* came up with several things, none of which seemed relevant, but I made a note:

Society for Preservation of Amplitude Modulation (physics stuff – maybe related?)
Society for the Protection and Advancement of Metroids
Society for Philosophy and Animal Minds
Society for the Preservation of American Modernists

And those were the least-weird ones.

I kept clicking all the way to page 10 on Google but nothing jumped out at me – it was all so very random. Then I figured maybe the A stood for Association, so I googled that. Apart from several anti-spam associations, I found the State Police Association of Massachusetts and a Facebook group called the Anti Pedro Spam Association, *to stop the spamming menace Pedro.* So, still all rubbish then.

I couldn't see what the P or M might stand for. Maybe my acronym idea was stupid. I tried Googling *I received an email from spam* – no interesting results, as you can imagine; *joining spam* – still nothing. The word spam had utterly lost all sense of meaning for me now. Those four letters looked like they should never be allowed to associate. I'd successfully broken my brain. I slapped my pillow in annoyance.

A few seconds later, Emma padded in.

Me: Knocking! Hello! Have you heard of it?

Emma: [totally ignoring me] Why are you making all that noise?

Me: I'm not making any noise.

Emma: Yes, you are. You're shouting and hitting things.

Me: I'm trying to help my friend, but I can't find what I'm looking for on Google.

Emma: Isn't everything on Google?

Me: That's the problem, actually. There are too many things on Google, and I think what I'm looking for is lost somewhere in the mess.

Emma: What is it that you are looking for?

Me: It's a company that sent an email to one of my friends. I'm trying to find out about them.

Emma: Maybe it's a secret company and they don't want people to find them?

Me: You're probably right. That's why I *want* to find them though. To figure out why they want to keep secret.

Emma: What is the email about?

Me: They just say that they want to meet up with him.

Emma: Can I look?

She'd got an adventurous glint in her eyes. I swivelled the laptop round to face her and told her the name I was looking for. She typed it in laboriously. That girl lives with a tablet glued to her fingers but give her a real keyboard and suddenly it's like she's a secretary on her first touch-typing class.

She pressed enter and the third entry on the results page jumped out at me:

UK-based hacking community SPAM

'What – how did you do that?!' I spluttered.

Then I noticed that the search words she'd typed in were *sp am comanty*. Somehow, her typo garbage had serendipitously led to something that seemed like it was exactly what I'd been looking for. I squeezed her hard in excitement and she squealed at me to get off. She was pretty excited too, though. I clicked on the link and scanned the page. It was a short article written on a low-quality news site with garish lettering and pop-up ads everywhere:

SPAM is an anarchist hacking community started by Brit Spencer Ambrose and named after him, using the first two letters of both his first and last names: SPencer AMbrose – SP AM – SPAM. It is notable for the skill of its members and the absolute secrecy they have been able to maintain, despite the group's longevity and size: over the two decades since it was formed, SPAM has grown to include members from all over the world, but the bulk of the community is still thought to reside in the UK.

SPAM funds itself through large money-making schemes, such as hacking into casino computer systems or phone providers. The bulk of their work is disruptive for disruption's sake, with no clear motive or aim other than to cause chaos. For example, they might launch attacks against companies in any sector, or politicians of any party and in any country.

Their attacks go from the facile, like hacking into a political website to make it display lewd messages, to the violent, such as breaking into the network used by the military, which resulted in a botched operation in Iraq causing six deaths to the British side.

Very little is known about SPAM's members, who can be of any age, gender and profession. No one has ever seen a picture of Ambrose's face, though this surveillance camera still is believed to be of him.

[There was a grainy photo of a man in a dark coat and hat, whose face wasn't visible at all].

I turned round to Emma. 'Emma, you're amazing – I think this is it!'

She had been reading over my shoulder with wide eyes. 'Clara, these people sound really bad! I don't think your friend should meet them.'

'Yup, and that was exactly what I was trying to find out.'

'What's that?' Emma asked, pointing at the screen. It was the spiral drawing that had been on the email from SPAM in Oli's inbox. Below the spiral, the legend read: *The Fibonacci spiral, which SPAM sometimes use in lieu of a logo, or to sign their work.*

'I don't know exactly, I said. 'It's some mathematical object but I haven't heard of it before.'

'Hmm,' Emma looked pensive. 'I am not in the mood for another one of your maths lessons right now,' she declared.

I burst out laughing. 'I'm not in the mood either,' I agreed. 'Hey thanks for your help, sis. Maybe when you're older we can set up a detective agency.'

'No thanks,' she said decisively, and hopped off the bed and back to her room.

I looked up a bit more about Spencer Ambrose. The more I read about him, the more I felt certain this had to be the right guy. He only recruited, very carefully and secretly, people who had made some waves in the hacking world already. He'd been known to be threatening if he wanted you to join. Everything I read was conjecture and gossip, but it's widely thought that he convinced one man to work for the organisation by getting his teenage son added to the list of suspects in a rape case. And I don't know if he goes out of his way to protect anyone who joins SPAM if they get in trouble either: Spencer himself has never been convicted of anything, but someone who was thought to be working for him got two years on probation for using a mobile phone free for several months.

Given the list of high-profile hacking jobs attributed to SPAM, though, that's a pretty small number of convictions.

Well – if the list I saw was correct. A few of them were noted as being possibly related to other groups. Spencer seems to be very happy to make cryptic statements or just stay silent whenever anything he is supportive of is attributed to SPAM. He has, however, come out twice to distance his organisation from hacking attacks: once, fifteen years ago, when a Casino in Nevada was hacked into and subsequently had to close down (Spencer called the hacking job an 'unsophisticated effort') and once when SPAM was floated as one of the possible hackers into the 2016 US election.

I grabbed my phone. Ty would be just getting out of school. I called him, and he picked up immediately. 'Ty! Iknowwhospamis!' My mouth seemed to have forgotten which movements to make to form actual words and instead just came out with a stream of random-sounding noise.

Ty paused. 'What?'

'Sorry,' I enunciated. 'I know who SPAM is.'

'What?! Oh my god – what?! How did you find out? Who are they?'

I filled him in on everything.

'Wow,' he exclaimed, 'you really found them!' He paused. 'But there's no way Oli would want to work with this group. He doesn't like working with other people in the best of situations, so why would he want to do it with this awful-sounding Spencer guy?'

'It's true that he never answered that email they sent him,' I pointed out.

'Yeah. It looks like he wasn't interested and just ignored them. Maybe that's why he left in fact – to get away from them after they got in contact!' He was thinking aloud, his voice excited again. 'From what you found, it looks like Spencer can be pretty... convincing. I'd certainly want to escape that if I was in Oli's shoes.'

'So you think Oli's in hiding from SPAM?'

'Yeah, it makes total sense!' Ty said. 'It would explain why he hasn't been messaging anyone. I mean, SPAM is a group of super-hackers, they could probably find him if he sent out any messages.'

He sounded relieved, like he'd convinced himself this was definitely what had happened. I didn't say anything. There were still a lot of unknowns. I wasn't even sure what would be better: for Oli to have joined a violent hacking group, or to be in hiding from them... neither of these options seemed particularly pleasant to me.

'Hey,' Ty said,' interrupting my thoughts. 'Are you still free to come over tonight?'

'Yes,' I said. My heart had been doing the I-found-SPAM dance for the past few minutes, but it immediately went back to the what-does-Ty-want-to-talk-about dance.

'Ok, great,' Ty said. 'Ok. I'll – I'll see you then.'

We hung up, and I decided to check all my bottles of nail polish to see which ones have gone gloopy in an effort to distract myself until a parent came home (it didn't work that great).

Thursday 13th October again – late

OH
MY
GOD

Oh my god. Oh my god. Oh my god!

I've just got back from Ty's. I…

Wow, my writing is a mess from all the excitement.

Um, deep breath. Where shall I start? At the beginning, I guess…

No. Let's start at the end.

I have had sex. I repeat, I have had SEX!

Right – *now* let's start at the beginning.

John came home around 5:30, with still no sign from Mum.

'I really need to work,' he whined, as if being a banker was on par with being a doctor. 'There's been a serious breach. It's a madhouse, honestly. My phone is ringing non-stop.' He pointed at his phone, which was indeed ringing. 'Do you think you could make some food quickly before you leave? It would really help me.'

'I can't. I have something important to do and I've been stuck here all day,' I said. 'Sorry,' I added as an afterthought, and skipped out, leaving him and his progeniture to it.

I was wearing my Salomon trainers and red cord trousers from one of the Camden vintage shops. I bought them with M – she forced me to haggle for them even though I hate doing it, so they only cost me £8. On top I wore a red skinny-strap tank, and then a black cashmere turtleneck over that. This is the exact outfit that I was wearing last time I went to the cinema with M, but it still took me 37 minutes and four outfit changes to get there. I was feeling nervous getting ready, and I couldn't even explain exactly why.

Of course, the spot I always get just above my left eyebrow had decided to make an appearance, and I couldn't get the concealer right. In the end I washed it all off and put on my brightest red lipstick. I convinced myself that the spot really brought the look together.

I took the bus to Ty's and texted him when I was at the door downstairs to his. He came down to open it for me.

'Hi,' I said. I felt weirdly shy coming over without the answer to a question ready.

'Hi,' he said back. 'Come in.'

I walked up the steps in front of him. He'd left the door to his apartment cracked open so I pushed it and walked to his bedroom. I realised that I felt at home at his place. Some people's homes are like that – things feel natural there, like you could open the fridge or pour yourself some water, or take off your shoes, without feeling awkward about any of it.

I sat on his bed as always. Ty was unusually silent. I could hear the cars driving down his street, honking, people talking and laughing and shouting outside. They felt very far away, or like they were just a movie soundtrack. And Ty, next to me, felt very close and very real.

He finally opened his mouth again. 'It's so great that you found who SPAM are,' was what he said.

Ok then, that wasn't quite as exciting as I'd hoped this conversation would be. 'Oh, yes,' I said. 'I think we're starting to understand what was going on with Oli before he left.'

'Did you find anything... like, any recent stories about them? I haven't had time to look yet.'

'Nothing that jumped out,' I said. 'But most of the stories about them are just people speculating, no one really knows what the truth is.'

Ty nodded absentmindedly. There was a long pause. Oh my god! Were we going to get stuck in a loop of useless conjecture about SPAM, not talking about the *something else*? My mouth seemed to be on conversation autopilot, so this could go on for hours if no one stopped it!

I opened my mouth again to break the silence but so did Ty.

'Maybe it's—'

'So I—'

We started laughing. The awkwardness that had lingered in the room since last night finally cracked a bit. 'You go,' I said. 'I wasn't going to say anything interesting.'

'Ok,' he smiled. 'Mine might be interesting. Or not.' He bit his lip and dove in. 'I wanted to see you because… um, I feel like I made yesterday a bit awkward and I really didn't want to leave it like that.'

I stayed silent, holding my breath.

'Things hadn't been going great with Alice for a while. Actually, they were only ever great right at the beginning, when I really think about it. And now, with this thing with Oli… well, I haven't even told her about it. I mean, she knows I'm worried about Oli being gone, but that's it. And I realised that I didn't *want* to talk to her about it at all. Whenever she asked me, I'd just change the subject. And so I guess that made it clear to me that we shouldn't be together anymore.' He looked up. 'So I wanted to tell you that it's not because of you – I mean, no wait, it *is* because of you.' He swallowed. 'What I'm trying to say is that we should have broken up a long time ago. But the reason I did it now is because... well, you're the only person I want to talk to these days, really.'

I sat there dumbstruck, as Ty obviously waited for me to demonstrate that I was a sentient being worthy of this declaration. Eventually he gave up and started talking again.

'So, um, yesterday, I was going to say this to you, but then you told me about, well, that you have a boyfriend. I didn't know that before, I mean, I had never seen you with anyone so I just sort of assumed that you... didn't have a boyfriend. I mean, not that I think you wouldn't have a boyfriend, or a girlfriend, or... never mind.' He shook his head. 'I guess I wanted to say sorry if I made things weird, which I really don't want to happen. You're doing so much to help me, and you're an amazing friend, and I just wanted you to... to know everything that's in my head. You can just ignore it all if you want. I know this is stupid timing. I mean, just after you tell me you have a boyfriend?' He smiled sheepishly. 'That got me by surprise, for sure. I thought... I mean, I thought you liked me...'

And then... I kissed him! KISSED him! It was pretty much exactly like I had imagined it. He smelt like soap and when I ran my hands in his hair it was soft and thick like you'd expect shampoo-commercial hair to feel. We kissed so hard it was as if weeks of kissing were trying to cram into one moment. His lips were full and a tiny bit dry, the sexy type of dry, making it tingle when he kissed my neck.

'I do like you,' I said quietly when we paused to take a breath.

'Yeah, I think I got that,' he laughed.

He stood up and pulled me to my feet, guiding me towards his bedroom as we kept kissing. His hands were all over me right away. I wanted to take all my clothes off and feel him so badly that it made breathing hard, and at the same time I couldn't stop seeing images in my head of Alice and him having sex, learning a million tantric sex tricks together while I still hadn't touched a penis not through fabric, even with the tip of my little finger.

We tumbled into his bedroom and he closed the door behind us with one arm. He slipped my jumper over my head in what would have been a practiced movement if it wasn't for the fact that turtleneck jumpers have obviously been designed by someone who is very against the very idea of getting undressed. We giggled a bit as I stood there faceless for a moment, ensconced in the jumper, until he tugged at it hard.

The kissing resumed. It was Hollywood-grade kissing. My hands explored under his T-shirt, where his skin was smooth like a dolphin. He pulled the T-shirt over his head from the back of the neck, in that careless way boys do which completely ruins their clothes. I tried to chase this stupid thought away, but in its place came Alice and her sex expert ways.

Then Ty kissed me again, and everything became electric. He slid his fingers lightly up my arm and to the nape of my neck, and then back down again, taking the strap of my top down with them. I jolted.

'Wait, Ty... there's something I need to... I'm, um... I haven't had sex before,' I mumbled, pulling the strap back up.

'Oh,' he breathed. 'I'm so sorry, I just assumed...'

'Yes. Well, we... I've done some stuff you know, but never, like... the whole thing.'

'We can do just... stuff, if you want,' Ty said softly. 'Or nothing, we can do nothing.'

'No, no. I want to. I really want to. Have sex with you. It's just...' Well, I couldn't very well tell him I was scared I'd do it all wrong and he would die laughing as his erection shrivelled away and then tell everyone at school, could I? 'I just wanted you to know.'

'Ok,' he said. 'But you can tell me. If you change your mind.'

He leant in to kiss me, all gentle like I was made out of tissue paper. I felt deflated. The electricity was crackling off.

'Don't do that,' I said.

'Do what?'

'Treat me like I'm fragile.'

'Sorry.'

'I'm not fragile.'

'Got it.'

'Besides, I've had sex plenty. In my head.'

Ty raised an eyebrow. 'With me?'

'With you. And Timothée Chalamet. Not at the same time though.'

He giggled.

'But seriously,' I said, 'just keep going like before I told you.'

'Well ok,' Ty said softly. 'Before you told me, I was doing this…'

He caught the strap of my top with his fingers again and pulled it slowly off my shoulder. The electricity crackled back on slightly. He kissed the place where the strap had been. More sparks. He pulled on the strap so that my top slipped off my breast and kissed down to there. Then he licked my nipple.

Oh. My. God.

I had no idea it would feel like that! It was like there was a thread going directly from my nipple to my vagina. For a moment, I forgot completely about everything in the world except for what was happening right then. I forgot I was nervous, I forgot about Alice. I certainly forgot about Sam (he'd been hovering extremely close by through all this, though I attempted to banish him by promising the goddess of bad decisions that I would be breaking up with him as soon as I next saw him next). I forgot about it all.

I had this sudden incredible, body-consuming need to feel something – to be clear, preferably one of Ty's body parts – inside me. It was such a strong feeling that it was almost painful. How weird is it that your body can feel that way? I guess it's some sort of biological imperative. I wondered what the corresponding feeling was like for Ty. I grabbed at him almost without thinking, just wanting to get closer. I grasped at the buttons of his fly.

Let's be honest, it was less smooth sailing from there. Fumbling with his buttons made my senses return – why are flies so impossible to work out on someone else? He ended up undressing himself, and then my trousers took some effort on both our parts to take off, getting stuck on my heels. I wished we were doing this in the summer, with easy-access skirts and dresses you tear off over your head. Alice returned, haunting me with her evident superhuman ability to take her clothes off without falling over herself.

We each pulled our socks off quickly, which felt decidedly non-Hollywood-y. Then Ty pulled his boxers down and there it was, standing at an angle I hadn't quite expected, my first full view of a real-life penis. I put my hand around it lightly, feeling nervous that I was going to do something wrong.

'Wow,' Ty said, and his breathing accelerated.

I squeezed a bit more and moved my hand up and down a little. He made a soft moan. Things were looking good. I was unsure where to go from there, but he grabbed my wrist suddenly.

'Wait. Slow down,' he said hoarsely.

I detached my hand and he turned around, opened the top drawer of his dresser and fumbled around for something. His arm came back out, hand clutching a condom. I sat down on the bed and he sat next to me.

'Umm… this isn't me treating you like you're fragile, I promise,' he said. 'But you're still ok?'

'Yes,' I answered. 'Keep going.'

I felt a bit annoyed that he'd asked after I'd told him I was fine, but I felt comforted too. And then I felt annoyed at myself for being comforted by him asking. And then I felt even more annoyed that my mind was off having these thoughts instead of leaving me to enjoy what was going on.

Anyway. He knelt in front of me at the foot of the bed and pulled my underwear off slowly. He kissed the inside of my calves, making everything go tingly, and started kissing his way up. I was... not ready for the kissing to get any higher – it seemed too many new things to feel nervous about and by now I was definitely nervous. And horny.

I grabbed his hair and pulled him up towards me. I sort of just wanted to get it over with. I wished I could fast-forward to when I would be doing this not for the first time.

'I really want to feel you inside me,' I whispered, hoping I sounded sexy.

He squeezed his eyes shut and let out a small moan. He stood up quickly, rolled the condom on and lay back down on top of me, his arms on either side of me. 'Tell me if it hurts, ok?' he said. 'I'll just stop'.

He pushed himself into me slightly. It felt good. Like, amazingly good. I heard a weird noise come out of my mouth. Ty looked at me quizzically.

'It's good. That was a good sound. Go on,' I told him.

He pushed a bit more. Suddenly, something hurt. Like, a lot. I gritted my teeth and didn't say anything. I wasn't about to ask him to stop after that speech about not being fragile. It stopped hurting pretty quickly, but I couldn't quite get back into the feeling I'd had before the... *penetrative sex*, as they call it in the doctor pamphlets. The thinking and the pain had taken me out of the moment.

Ty moved back and forth over me, breathing hard. I liked feeling his hot breathing right in my ear. I relaxed a bit and I started to feel both our bodies moving together like they had agreed a secret rhythm. Then after a little while – I honestly could not tell you how long – he buried his face in the pillow and seemed to shudder all over from the inside. That was amazing actually, the thought that I had made him feel that way. It made me feel like kissing him again, but I didn't move because he was just laying still and he was quite heavy.

He stayed like that for a bit and then rolled over, peeled the condom off, made a knot in it and dropped it by the bed. It was pretty obvious that he'd made that gesture a lot of times before. Alice sauntered back before my eyes, telling me that of course he'd done it a million times before, with *her*.

Ty rolled back over to lie on his back next to me. I turned onto my side and rested my hand on his chest. I could feel a few drops of sweat running down my neck, his sweat, or mine, or a mixture. I liked how mixed up our bodies now were, like there were bits of him in me and bits of me in him.

'That was incredible,' he said. 'Um, I know that it didn't feel as good for you? Like... finishing? But you'll show me. Next time, you can show me what you like. Oh, wait,' He put his hands over his eyes. 'There doesn't have to be a next time. I mean, if you don't want.'

I started to laugh, and then he started to laugh.

'Wow, what a time we live in,' I said.

'Yeah. Take me back to the Middle Ages, please.'

'We'd be married by now.'

'So much simpler,' he sighed.

I looked at him. 'I do want there to be a next time,' I told him.

'Oh good,' he said. 'Phew. I just... I know that it's confusing with the stuff with my brother as well. I don't want it to feel like the two are... mixed up, or anything.'

'I don't feel mixed up,' I said. 'I want to help you, and I also want to do... this.'

'Ok.' He smiled, a real happy smile. 'Ok, ok.'

We didn't have sex again but we lay on the bed together and his hands did a little random dance over my body as we talked. We'd put like half our clothes back on. His fingers trailed on my skin absentmindedly and I never knew where they were going next. It was really turning me on, actually, but I didn't know how to convey that fact, so I just stewed in my horniness.

When I had to go, Ty walked me downstairs and into the dark. I had been feeling really comfortable and relaxed with him, but the second the door closed behind me I got a horrible gnawing in my stomach, which hasn't eased up since. I've just cheated on the loveliest-ever boy. I am a *cheater*. Even when I break up with Sam when I see him tomorrow, that fact won't change.

Back at home, it looked like John had let Emma eat cereal for dinner. I could hear him on the phone in the office. I climbed upstairs and had a hot shower which felt incredible. There was a little bit of blood in my underwear, but not much. It was less red-torrent-of-shame-from-the-movies and more day-minus-one-of-my-period. I washed my pants out in the sink to ward off any chance of a grilling from Mum and threw them into the laundry basket.

| 5 |

Sizes of Infinity... Plus Some Irrationality!

Friday 14th October

Well of course, yesterday evening, as soon as I finished writing, I called M. She didn't answer, but I texted her that I'd had *SEX*, in capitals. *Penis in vagina*, I added, to be clear. She called back within 11 seconds.

So. I told her everything. She gasped and oohed in all the right places. I told her about Ty, about Alice; I told her about Oli and the computer: everything. It felt so good telling her, like I'd had some awful heavy monster sitting on my shoulders, slapping me around the head relentlessly, and suddenly it was gone. It was so good also to tell her how nervous I felt about Oli and SPAM. I don't feel like I can really say everything I'm thinking to Ty because obviously he's scared himself and so I have to be the one who stays calm. Though M perhaps wasn't the best person to say it to either, given that she is prone to extreme drama and was immediately imagining doom scenarios far beyond mine.

When it came to the having-sex part, however, she was much more reasonable. Well, a little more reasonable. 'Do you feel any different?' she asked. 'Are you super mature now?'

'No,' I mused. 'I don't feel different at all.'

I unconsciously touched parts of my body, where Ty had touched them. Everything felt just the same as before, except some soreness and, if I'm honest, some muscle pain in areas that I don't think had ever been exercised before. As for inside my brain, there was definitely no fresh clarity to report. 'In fact I'm probably less mature than ever, just keep messing things up,' I told M. My stomach had a Sam-shaped pain inside it.

'What a disappointment. I thought I had extra maturity to look forward to.'

'It would be a disappointment, except it felt very good.'

'No orgasm, though,' she sniffed.

'I'll make sure to give Ty your feedback,' I laughed. 'I think he was going to... you know, with his tongue. But I didn't feel ready for that.'

'You stopped him from going down on you? Why would you do that?! Apparently it's the best thing!'

'I'm sorry, hopefully I'll have better things to report next time,' I promised.

M's voice went serious. 'I'm so happy you finally decided to tell me what's been going on,' she said.

'I'm so, so sorry I didn't tell you before,' I practically wailed.

'Hey,' she said soothingly, 'you'd promised Ty. I get it.'

'You seemed so pissed off with me and it made me feel horrible.'

'I wasn't pissed off with you,' M said. 'I mean, I was a bit, but it wasn't because of you not telling me stuff, it was... you were being really self-absorbed.'

'I was, I really was. I never even tried to see how it would feel from your side. I never wondered what you might imagine was going on. '

'It's more that you didn't...' she paused. 'You didn't notice that I needed you.'

'You needed me?' I got a sinking feeling in my stomach. 'Wait M, what happened?'

'It's...' she sighed again. 'Listen. Tomorrow after school, can you come to mine? I'd rather talk in person.'

'Yes. Yes, of course.'

We hung up and I texted Sam that I had to cancel seeing him and suggested Sunday instead. I'll be honest – at first, I was relieved. I had two whole extra days before I needed to think of what I would say to him. Then this morning I woke up to a heart from him in response to my messages, and I felt worse than before. Now I have to get through the whole weekend before I can break up with him. What was I thinking? This is way worse than doing it right away. A whole weekend of turning things round and round in my head.

Saturday 15th October

Slept at M's last night, curled up in her single bed like when we were younger. She kicks and starts in her sleep and makes me wake up in a panic every couple of hours – and of course, she stays deeply asleep all the way through it. It used to drive me mad. Sometimes I'd pour a glass of water on her face in retaliation, though she's even slept through that. I've given up over the years, I just accept it now.

After school I went over to hers and she came out to hug me. We walked around for a bit. She asked for more sex details, which I gladly gave her, but I could tell that she was gathering up courage to tell me what she wanted to. I felt apprehensive. M normally talks *before* she does any thinking. Finally, I figured she might need a little encouragement.

'M, tell me what happened,' I said softly.

She paused. 'Sorry. I didn't know how to start.'

'Just start now,' I said. 'And don't apologise when you don't need to.'

'That's what I always say to you,' she pointed out.

'I know,' I said.

M fidgeted, twiddling at her ring. 'It's about Leo...'

'The guy who works with your mum?' I asked, getting worried.

'Yes. He... after we met, he called me. It felt so grown up for someone to actually call, you know? Because all the other guys just send a text asking what's up and then nothing more for days. So when Leo called I was like, ok, *this* is what's up. We had such an easy conversation too, it was like I'd known him forever. He said —' She looked sideways at me. 'You're going to roll your eyes so hard,' she groaned, and hid her face with her hands.

'What?'

'He said he wanted to photograph me. He does these, like, aura photographs. It's a special camera from the '70s. It captures the electromagnetic field around you. His dad had one that was broken, and he restored it. The aura shows up as all these colours on the photo. Anyway, he said... He said that he really wanted to see what my aura was because he'd never met anyone like me.'

'You're right, I *am* rolling my eyes.'

'The photo came out so beautifully though,' she protested.

She took something out of her pocket to show me. It was a polaroid photo that showed her sitting, looking very peaceful, with smiling eyes even though her face was at rest. She was surrounded by a yellow and purple haze. It was genuinely gorgeous.

'He said he'd never seen yellow and purple like that before, so...'

'What do the colours mean?' I asked.

'Yellow is, like, openness. Purple is unconventional.'

I raised my eyebrows. 'Ok, so he has a magic camera that can see your soul. I am starting to get the appeal. Why didn't you tell me about all this?'

'You were so obsessed with his age when I first told you about him, so I didn't want to go into it. And after that, well, you were acting weird...'

I squeezed her hand. 'I'm sorry I'm sorry,' I said. 'Never will I ever do that again. What happened?'

'Well, he suggested on the phone that we do the photo on Sunday, and we kept talking for ages and also every day until then, so by the time I went over there it was like we'd known each other forever. Everything felt really easy. He set up the shot, took the photo and after we watched it develop on the polaroid film, he told me what the colours meant and then he kissed me. He was an incredible kisser. Dreamy. We were kissing and talking; he showed me some other photographs he'd taken and then I spotted a flyer on the table. It was for his show coming up in a few days. I said it looked really cool and I'd come and he made this weird, awkward face and was like, don't come actually, because there's this girl I met in Berlin who is flying over and she will be there.'

'Ah.'

'Yeah. I felt a bit gross about it, but I said I still wanted to come. He said no and I promised I wouldn't make it weird or anything. He started raising his voice and said that if I couldn't respect his boundaries then this wouldn't work.'

'What an asshole!' I interjected.

M sighed. 'Yeah. I mean, I guess I was being a bit pushy. I told him that I thought I *was* respecting his boundaries and I wouldn't act like anything other than a friend at the show, but that I found it pretty disrespectful to outright tell me not to come.'

'Exactly,' I concurred, feeling righteous.

'Well, he didn't agree. He yelled at me and called me petulant. Said he'd been wrong and that I wasn't mature at all, that I had to learn that I don't get to do whatever I want to all the time in the real world. That I was just a kid using my tits and my pussy to pretend she was a grown-up. That's what he said. He backed me up against the wall and said, "You think you're all grown up, do you? Just because you wave your tits and pussy in my face and you feel proud of the effect you have." And when he said it, he sort of – grabbed at them. At my breasts and between my legs. As if they were just... things.'

'Oh my god...' I breathed.

'I stood there frozen for a split second and then I ran the hell out of there. I made it round the corner and then I just – I cried.'

'Oh. M,' I said. I put my arm around her waist. M never cries.

'No one paid me any attention until this sweet old grandma walked past me and she stopped and pulled a tissue out of her bag for me. She said, "He's not worth it, I promise – a beautiful girl like you can get any boy she wants." It actually worked. I mean, not what she said, but I couldn't bear the thought that I was such a cliché. Dried the tears right up.' She cracked a little laugh. 'Then I called you a few times, but you didn't answer,' she added.

I threw both my arms around her neck and kissed her gorgeous face. 'I am so, so sorry that I was not there for you, and that I was acting weird and you didn't feel you could tell me about it,' I said. 'You should always tell me everything that happens. Even if I'm being shitty.'

'I know. I mean, I was upset with you, but mainly... I was a bit embarrassed, I guess. You told me right away not to get involved.'

I shrugged. 'What do I know?'

'More than me, evidently.'

We walked in silence for a couple of minutes, our steps falling into line with each other.

'You know,' I said, 'what he did is really not ok... Touching you like that.'

'Positively Trumpian,' M agreed.

'I'm not joking, M. Just imagine how you would feel if it had happened to me.'

'I'd have ripped his penis off already,' she admitted. 'Clara – I thought about telling my mum, I really did. But she thinks he's great, says the kids at the centre love him and he's made a real difference there... I don't know. I don't want to ruin it all for them.'

I sighed. 'If you ever decide to tell her what happened, I'll be right there with you, ok?'

'I already feel so much better just having talked about it with you,' M said. 'I don't even know how to explain the way it made me feel. Sort of like I wasn't a person, you know? Like someone could decide it was fine to do whatever they wanted to me. I guess – I thought that I could deal with anything in the world. I've had loads of guys be gross to me on the street, and it doesn't even phase me, I just shout right back at them. I thought I was invincible. And then, I don't know – this tiny thing happens and it's like it created a huge crack in my invincible shield.'

'It wasn't tiny. And it's fine not to be invincible.'

M burst out laughing. 'I was thinking more that I'm going to kintsugi that shit up and get invincible again.'

I rolled my eyes. 'Yeah right, you do that, and in the meantime you just make sure you talk to me about *everything*.'

I held her hand tight as we walked all the way back to hers.

Sunday 16th October

This diary-writing isn't going at all how I thought it would. I thought Ty and me would be brilliantly solving the mystery of Oli's disappearance and I'd be celebrating our triumph in these pages within a handful of days, in a witty and breathless recounting. Instead, we still haven't solved anything, Oli is more disappeared than ever with two new mysteries in the form of GCHQ and SPAM, and my journal has become a repository for relationship angst. And today's offering is truly overflowing.

First of all, there is M's story and the things I dream of happening to that vile guy. The dreaming in question is both daydreaming and night dreaming – I had a very violent night's sleep.

Then there's Mum who was acting extremely weird last night, texting on her phone the whole time. Eventually she walked into the TV room and closed the door behind her. A minute later, I heard her voice mumbling through the wall. She'd closed the door to make a phone call? I crept closer and tried to listen, but the words were too muffled. I could hear, though, that what had started out calm was escalating a bit and then it ended abruptly. Was she arguing with John? She didn't usually bother doing that in private. Was she arguing with… Dad? She had mentioned something about being out in the evening, and now that was clearly not happening.

Then, there's the fact that Ty didn't text me at all on Saturday, which I was too busy to notice because I was with M. But by now, 3pm on Sunday, he still hasn't written. I've got to the stage when I am obsessively stalking all his social media for clues. He barely posts anything and when he does it's either about football or some arty photo he took, which doesn't help my stalking at all.

I am starting to feel stressed about it. Maybe he's changed his mind about me? I thought it had gone well on Thursday, but what if it was actually awful? What if he was pretending to enjoy it, and then he was just nice to me because he needs me to keep working on the maths questions? Maybe he's regretting everything right now and doesn't know what to do.

Finally, obviously, there's Sam. I have to leave in an hour to go and see him and break up, and my heart has been in my throat all day about it. It's like there are two completely separate Claras: the one that had sex with Ty feels so strange and remote right now and yet she's me. She's bullying the other me, the one that is going to see Sam.

I've tried getting ready for it – thinking about what I'm going to say exactly, even writing a script. But every time I start picturing his face it's like my brain suddenly shuts down and instead, I'm sorting the books on my shelf by alphabetic order or Marie Kondo-ing my jewellery with tears prickling my eyes. I just can't believe that after I do this he won't be there anymore. I literally cannot imagine what it's going to be like – his existence has always been a background to whatever I do in my life.

It reminds me of how I felt before Grandpa died: how weird it was, going to visit him in hospital. It always felt so normal being there and he would be so *himself* and yet I knew that I was supposed to feel that these visits were special somehow, that I should be *making the most of them,* whatever that meant. It wasn't until he did actually die that I got it – the great big hole it left. I mean, not that Sam's dying or anything. God, I'm being so stupid comparing a break-up with someone being gone forever. I mean, he'll still exist and maybe we can stay friends. We'll still be there for each other and we can just celebrate our birthdays by drinking too much like normal people, instead of inventing stupid adventures for ourselves.

Lots of people manage to stay friends with their exes and Sam is just about the nicest person in the whole world. If anyone can make it work, it's him! He'll probably be grateful I'm breaking up with him. He won't have to put up with me being moody and unsure anymore. He'll be free to go out with other, much nicer, fully committed people. No – wrong thought, wrong thought – that makes me want to not go through with it...

M and I discussed it this morning. I knew that she would be fully supportive, considering her lack of enthusiasm for Sam. To my surprise though, she was not at all as jubilant as I expected. She wasn't jubilant at all, really. She told me to call her right after and she'd come over if needed. Nice, but unhelpful in terms of giving me courage.

I'm going to work on Oli's question until I have to leave – at least this way I am not entirely wasting my life.

Secret question: Are there more rational or irrational numbers?

It's easy to find the definition of rational and irrational numbers. A rational number is one you can express as a fraction, so like 2/3 or 56/87 or 187/5, or any fraction at all. And an irrational number is the opposite – one that you can't express as a fraction.

It turns out that, if you write them all out as decimals, the rational numbers are the ones that either don't have an infinite number of digits after the decimal, like 3.6578, or they do have an infinite number of digits after the decimal, and a pattern develops in the digits somewhere along the line, like -2.35353535... or 6.15790573573573573...

The irrational numbers are the other ones, the ones that have an infinite number of digits after the decimal, with no pattern ever developing. 0.13546795852899477... is a good start, though obviously, unless I write out all the digits (not going to do that because I don't have infinity time on my hands) you can't know if a pattern ever starts happening down the line.

What I don't understand is that there is an infinite number of both, so I really don't see how there could me more of one type than the other. I personally know way more rational numbers than irrational ones (I looked up some examples of irrational numbers – $\sqrt{2}$ and π are both irrational, which apparently made the Greeks really angry when they understood it, because before then they'd thought that all numbers were rational, which is a lot less messy), so maybe there are more rational numbers? It's actually quite hard to think of an example of an irrational number.

I have to stop now. It's 4pm and I need to leave. I've purposefully picked a bad outfit and haven't washed my hair so that Sam will feel lucky to get rid of me. Still no sign from Ty, so… off I go to take myself from two boys to probably zero.

Monday 17th October

Well. The past twenty-four hours have been a disaster. I guess '90s TV had it right – the second a girl has unmarried sex, the whole world implodes.

In Maths class this morning, Ty arrived just before the bell and barely looked at me. He glanced over with what could have been a half-smile or a grimace and then stared straight ahead of him.

Mr Howard surprised us with a quiz and I could barely think straight. I felt like every slight change in the back of Ty's neck or the slope of his shoulders was directed at me. I was sure that everyone in the class knew exactly what had happened between us – which turned out to be pretty much true, because in the afternoon I had the misfortune of bumping into Alice and Rayna in the hall.

Alice's eyes were rimmed with red and Rayna was patting her gently on the back. When Rayna spotted me, her eyes threw a million tiny daggers in my direction. I thought I would be smitten instantly and fall in a crumpled heap to the floor. That might even have been better than what did happen, which was that Rayna loudly called me a 'cheating slut' to the gleeful amazement of everyone in the vicinity.

I could feel my eyes burning and tears coming, and I really didn't want to give her the satisfaction of seeing that, so I pushed my way past them without saying anything, keeping my head down. Rayna stuck out a Stan-Smithed foot to trip me up like a mean girl from a high-school movie. I stumbled but thankfully didn't fall and marched away quickly, willing the tears to be sucked back into my face. Everyone stared and whispered.

When I was far away from them, I straightened up, feeling shaky and awful. Alice had stood quietly during the whole encounter. Her eyes didn't throw any daggers, just sadness. Pretty, damsel-in-distress, wet sadness. *I AM a cheating slut*, I thought.

I texted M to tell her what had happened, hiding in a bathroom stall, breathing slowly through my nose to calm down. *Slut-shaming is even more lame than Rayna's flat-ironed hair*, she texted back. I leaned my head against the gross bathroom wall, not even caring about the germs; a sure sign that things were bad. Yes, M always makes me feel better. But really, Rayna was more right than she could even guess. Because what happened with Sam yesterday was... well, imagine the worst way things could have gone, and then imagine worse than that.

I went over to his, right after I stopped writing the last entry. We sat in his back garden, which is completely sheltered from wind and was surprisingly warm in the sun. He was wearing my favourite soft green shirt of his, which made the matching green specks in his eyes stand out. I tried to hold out, sweating and suffocating in the heat, but I had to give up and take my sweatshirt off. Underneath I was wearing an old white tank that I often sleep in and no bra. I crossed my arms around my chest to hide the darker outlines of my nipples. Let's be honest, this was not an ideal way to start.

We talked about random stuff for a bit. My mind was so far from the conversation that I kept saying nonsense, like:

Sam: So what did you do over the weekend?

Me: [long pause] Sorry... what?

Sam: This weekend? What did you do?

Me: [long pause again] No.

Sam: What do you mean, "no"? You didn't have a weekend? You didn't do anything?

Me: Oh sorry! You mean what did I do this weekend?! [furiously trying to remember an example of an activity that doesn't involve being naked] Nothing much! I saw M! We had food!

Sam: [understandably puzzled] You had food? Like, any specific type of food?

Me: Yes, exactly.

I knew things were going badly. I kept trying to say something sensible, like, 'I've been thinking a lot about it and I feel like I am with you because I love you, but I am not in love with you anymore.' (That was the line I'd worked out on the way over). Or even just, 'We need to talk.' Everyone knows what that means, don't they? But none of that came out of my mouth. Instead I was battling with thoughts like, *But he is so sweet*, and, *Doesn't he look amazing in that shirt?* and, *Is his voice extra-smooth today?* and, *Ty is obviously never going to speak to me again anyway*, and, *Maybe I AM in love with Sam – I mean, I really, really like him, and is there actually a difference?*

'You're so distracted today,' he said, cutting through the voice in my head. 'What's up?'

And with that perfect opportunity... I kissed him.

Oh yes. I kissed him. And it wasn't just any kissing either. I kissed him urgently and passionately and all the words ending in -ly that I don't usually associate with Sam. Like, hair-grabbing, neck-biting, hands-everywhere kissing. Every time we came up for breath my brain started up like, *What are you doing?! Are you insane?? Stop it right now!* And every time, the easiest way to silence it was to get back to the kissing, which was, frankly, very pleasurable.

'Wow,' Sam said after a bit, creating space for my brain to start up again.

'Let's just do it – let's have sex now,' I said desperately, to shut it back down.

As soon as I said it, I thought, *Yes, that's what we need, we just got stuck doing the same thing again and again, forget the stupid birthday thing!* Yeah, I wasn't thinking straight. Also, I was horny. Turns out having sex makes you want to have sex more afterwards.

'Are you sure? We said we'd wait until our next birthday,' he whispered.

'Who cares?!'

'So you're really sure?'

'Yes!' I replied and grabbed his hand to shut him up. We went inside and climbed the stairs up to his bedroom.

'Ok, ok...' Sam looked around, dazed. He started flitting around the room, lifting things up and putting them back down frenetically. 'Where have I put the condoms??'

His shirt was half undone, showing off a patch of thin curly hair that has appeared on his chest in recent months. He was flushed bright red. His bedroom had that same faint smell it always does: a bit damp because it doesn't get a lot of air, mixed with cabbage from the soup his mum makes all the time.

'Um, maybe they're in your bedside table like always?' I said, sounding distinctly impatient.

Shit. I was feeling a lot less sure about my decision already. I mean, it didn't take much to realise that this was obviously a completely idiotic thing to do, but also I wasn't so into it anymore. The moment had gone flat.

Sam found the condoms and got one out of the box with febrile hands, placed it on top of his bedside table for easier access later and got back to the business of kissing me.

'Wow, I can't believe this is finally happening,' he said breathlessly. He gazed into my eyes tenderly. My chest constricted with guilt.

'Wait,' I said. I dropped to my knees. Anything to stop seeing him look at me like that.

I got his belt open quickly, undid his zipper and pulled down his jeans and his boxers. The light was very bright, and I got a good look at every single little hair and puckered bit of skin. There was a slight sweaty smell – not unlike the soup smell I guess, but a bit more... meaty. I wasn't exactly *dying* to put it in my mouth but when I did, Sam gasped and looked like he had been transported straight to whatever Jewish heaven is. He grabbed hold of the wall with one hand to steady himself and his other hand tangled in my hair uncontrollably. I got more into it as his breathing got heavier. It was pretty awkward and I was unclear on what to do with my tongue, but overall the whole blowjob thing was a lot less difficult than I had expected. Well, until—

'Um, if you keep going I'm going to – I'll – you know...' he gasped.

I kept going and about seven seconds later something tasting of over-ripe fruit filled my mouth. I stayed there frozen for a long-ish moment, squeezed my eyes shut and swallowed whole. Then I promptly burst into tears.

'Oh my god, are you ok?' Sam dropped to his knees and cupped my sobbing face in his hands.

I shook my head, willing the tears to stop. How awful! I am always crying at the worst moments. Paloma tells me her cat just died and I get a case of the giggles, but then I get fined for having the wrong ticket on the train and it's full-on waterworks in front of the ticket controller and the whole carriage. And now – here we were again. I wiped at the flood ineffectually with my hands and pulled away from Sam.

'Did I do something wrong?' he asked, looking concerned.

'No, that's not it!' I wailed, 'I... I had sex with someone else!'

Now, keep in mind that he was naked at that point. I was topless, with tears and snot running down my face. We were both crouching on the faded carpet. I could still taste what I had just swallowed on my tongue. The penis was just going back to soft... Picture the scene – can you imagine a worst possible setting for my declaration? Personally, I really could not. And I think Sam agreed.

For the first time in our lives, he got angry with me. He actually swore at me. I was almost transfixed because it was such an unusual sight, but then I remembered that the best thing I could do was just leave.

I picked up my top and sweatshirt off the floor and rushed downstairs carrying them as Sam slammed his bedroom door behind me. I got dressed quickly in his kitchen and ran practically all the way home. Then I let myself fall face-first onto my bed and cried all the way until this morning. And I've already gone over how this morning went, so there you have it: an utter and total disaster.

I think I need to call M again.

Monday 17th October - night

M remained surprisingly calm throughout my anguished phone call. She'd already had to do a heavy consoling session at school, so this time she tried a different tactic.

M: I think it's good that it went down the way it did with Sam. Now you can really put it behind you. Just think – if you hadn't done it now, then it would have happened when you're thirty-five, just had your second kid, husband is hiding away from his responsibilities at work and suddenly you're like, what if Sam really was the love of my life all along? Of course, he's still single and pining after you, and BAM!

Me: That's a nice life you're planning for me.

M: All right, you have an amazing husband, your kids are delightful, but you bump into Sam randomly one day and then you start wondering, *What if, what if?* And slowly, the *what ifs* creep into your head and... BAM! Again! You ruin your perfect life over a *what if.*

Me: Where are these scenarios coming from? Don't I have any better options? Preferably one where I don't have kids. Emma is not exactly a great advert for them.

M: Sorry, you're right. You do not need to live inside a daytime TV show. My point is that whatever happens, the unresolved Sam stuff would a problem, you see?

I laughed and shook my head. M had made me feel better. Not just her silliness, but also because she maybe had a point. Maybe it did need to happen at some time. Maybe things would have forever felt unfinished otherwise. Or maybe I'm just clutching at straws, to justify this thing I've done. Yeah, probably that.

M: Look, that's what's happening with your parents! You're genetically predisposed. What's happening with that, by the way, have you found out more?

Me: Ugh, please. I already have Dad's disproportionate torso and Mum's dancing with her hands in the air. Listen, I've been too distracted by everything to think about them, but yes I'm 98% certain that something is going on. Though the other night, I think – I *think* they had an argument.

M: Oh no…

Me: Honestly, M, if I'm right and that's what it was, it's really not surprising. They separated for a reason – it just didn't work between them. In fact, I don't think it *ever* really worked, not even in the beginning. They had fun and it was exciting and they were in love, sure, but literally every story they tell about those years is about some massive argument they had. You know, other parents have cute little stories about the beach where they went skinny-dipping together, but my parents have a story about *screaming at each other* on the beach and Dad almost drowning because he went swimming angry and kept going further than he intended. That's what they found romantic – making up after an argument because one of them nearly died. It was always either really amazing or totally awful with them, and the awful times had for sure taken over by the end. I promise, being their daughter became a far more relaxed and pleasant experience once they separated. They instantly started getting on better and it's only improved since then. Hence, I suppose, ironically, the current situation.

I could hear M's mum Amanda shouting in the distance: Miracle! I'm going to make some yoghurt. Do you want to help?

M: [shouting back] Make some yoghurt? Why don't you just buy some at the shop?!

Amanda: [not shouting anymore because she was now close by]. But this way I made it! It's fun!

M: It'll probably be disgusting.

Amanda: Oh, you're on the phone, sorry! Is that Clara?

M: Yes. Mum, remember when you tried to make kombucha? Just buy the yoghurt.

Amanda: Hi Clara!

Me: Hi Amanda!

It made me feel happy to hear them talking about silly things. At least something in my life was going better than before.

M: Ok, Mum, this is a very important conversation. Clara needs my expert opinion on something.

Amanda: Fine, I'll make the yoghurt on my own.

M: Buy the yoghurt, Mum. [She sighed]. Oh well. What were we talking about?

Me: Nothing. I should go actually, I guess.

M: Are you going to work on Oli's maths question?

Me: Yes. I mean, just in case Ty does decide to speak to me again.

I was definitely pouting. The thought of working on Oli's problem while things stood as they did with Ty made me feel lethargic.

Me: I'm really stuck with this one. It's never taken me this long before.

M: What does the question say?

Me: Are there more rational or irrational numbers.

M: Huh? What's that?

Me: It's... Oh, never mind. What I don't get is that there's an infinite number of each, so how can there be more of one of them?

M: Oh! But... I know about that!

Me: What?! You do?

M: Yeah! I mean, I don't know the answer to your question, but in Philosophy class, let me see... I remember that we were talking about how philosophers deal with situations when there are two different answers that could both be right – how do you pick which one you believe in? And then someone said that's why science is more relaxing – there's always a right answer. And then Ms Nguyen said something about sizes of infinity... Some mathematician who went crazy because of something to do with sizes of infinity.

Me: Oh my god! Who?

M: Ah, what was his name... Wait I'll get it, I promise! It was similar to the philosopher we were talking about, but I can't remember which one that was now. Nietzsche? Descartes? No –

Oh, it was Kant! The mathematician's name was Kanter, something like that.

Me: Ok... Kanter. And really, he went crazy because of sizes of infinity?

M: Yeah. I swear that was it!

Me: That sounds... It really sounds like this could be what I'm looking for!

I felt my heart racing. I was excited again. I remembered how great it felt to crack one of the questions on my own, Ty or no Ty. I was actually impatient to look up this Kanter person.

M said a quick goodbye, very pleased with her contribution.

I got my computer out and found him quite easily – not Kanter, but *Cantor*, Georg Ferdinand Ludwig Philipp Cantor, a German mathematician from the late 1800s, who did indeed finish his life in a sanatorium, having had a breakdown after people criticised one of his theories. I couldn't for the life of me understand what exactly that theory was, but it was something to do with whether he had in fact found how to describe all the possible sizes of infinity, or whether there were more sizes in between the sizes he'd found. Yeah.

The helpful bit came when I read an explanation of the first two sizes of infinity, which Cantor had written about in one of the very first articles he published. The smallest infinity is the one that contains all the whole numbers. It is called *countable infinity*, simply because it's the one that you can count. To count the whole numbers you just put them in order: 1, 2, 3, 4... You'll never be finished, because there are an infinite number of them, but you know that if you keep counting forever, you'll never miss one of them out.

Any set of things that is infinite but that you can put in a neat order like that is of countable infinity size. For example, the even numbers are countable infinity size – you can just put them in order of size 2, 4, 6, 8... And the whole numbers both positive and negative are a countable infinity too – you can put them in the order 0, 1, -1, 2, -2, 3, -3, 4, -4...

The next size up of infinity is the real numbers (so, all the decimal numbers on the number line). This is not countable: there is no way of ordering all the real numbers in a neat way so that you don't miss any of them out. It hurts my head a bit, but I can see that it makes sense – it feels like there are just 'too many' real numbers. If you think of a random decimal number, like 5.67953725410935392311... how would you decide which number should come just after it in your ordering? It's all much more messy than the whole numbers.

So I was ok with Cantor's first two infinities: countable infinity and real-numbers infinity. The real numbers are made out of the rational and the irrational numbers. Since they both go inside the real numbers, obviously they can't be a *bigger* infinity that the real numbers. And since the question asked which there were more of, they must be of different sizes of infinity, which means that one of them must be countable – ie one of them, either the rational numbers or the irrational numbers, can be put in a nice order.

At first glance this seemed impossible. I could hardly come up with any irrational numbers or think of writing them out, so how could I start thinking about how to order them?

And the rational numbers weren't any better – if I thought of a fraction, like 4/5, I could see no way of deciding which other fraction should go immediately after it in my order. I started to think of the possibilities: I could put 9/10 right after 4/5, but then I'd have to fit 13/15 in between them, and then I'd have to squeeze in 17/20 in the middle as well... I could go on like that forever!

I was thinking about it all wrong though, there's actually a really simple way of putting all the fractions in an order – you just need to forget about doing it in size order and instead think geometrically.

If you think of all the fractions in the world, the numerator can be any whole number, and the denominator can be any whole number as well. So you can represent all these fractions in an x,y grid where the numerator corresponds to the x-coordinate, and the denominator to the y-coordinate.

You end up with a grid that has a point representing a fraction at each intersection. Then you can just go through the whole grid, ticking the fractions off one by one as you go, zig-zagging diagonally, without ever missing any of them out.

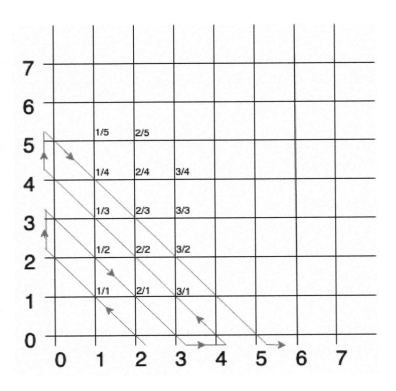

(Note that when you do this, you'll technically be counting the same number lots of times. For example, you'll first come up to 1/2, and then later on you'll get to 2/4, 3/6, etc, and these are all the same number. So if you want to be really precise about it, you have to do your zigzag ordering, but skip any fraction that is the same as one that's come before.)

This means that the fractions – the rational numbers – are countable, and so the irrational numbers are the size above of infinity. So even though I couldn't think of more than two irrational numbers, there are in fact way more of them than there are rational numbers.

I squealed to myself with joy and reached for my phone to tell Ty, before I abruptly remembered that he wasn't speaking to me.

Just then, as I was staring at my phone, my elation fading away, his name appeared as if I'd summoned him.

Me: Hello?

Ty: Clara, you picked up!

Me: Um, yes?

Ty: I just... You weren't speaking to me and listen, I get it, I made things complicated, and we can just forget—

Me: —I thought you weren't speaking to me!

Ty: What? Oh.

Me: [laughing] Yeah.

Ty: [also laughing] But... you looked so upset with me at school?

Me: I wasn't upset with you. It seems like Alice and her friends have found out.

Ty: They were giving you a hard time?

Me: Well. Yeah.

Ty: I'm so sorry, Clara. Alice is normally a really nice person, I swear. But she's super angry at me right now. I wish I could help more, get her to stop doing this to you.

Me: It's not really Alice anyway... Rayna is the one who was being awful.

Ty: Oh right. I've been on the receiving end of that and she can be really nasty, I know. She... I don't know if this helps at all, but I think she's in love with Alice.

Me: What?

Ty: Yeah. She told me at a party once when she was completely trashed. I found her throwing up in the loo and helped her clean up. She said she was jealous of me and all sorts of stuff. I don't think she remembers any of it – we've never talked about it since.

Me: Wow.

I started to feel bad for Rayna and her heart troubles, then I remembered that she'd made fun of that gay mayor in America for his statement about paternity leave, and all the times she'd found pretending that M and I were a couple to be the height of hilarity. I stopped feeling so bad.

Ty: Hey, I know I don't really have a right to ask you to keep another secret, but… I don't think she'd want anyone knowing. I just thought maybe it would make you feel better.

Me: Don't worry, I won't tell anyone. She's the worst but even horrible people should get to decide what other people know about their private life.

Ty: She's really not so horrible when you know her…

Me: Don't push it.

Ty: Fine, fine. So you're really, truly not upset about Thursday?

Me: Whatever the total opposite of upset is, that's what I am.

Ty: Ok… Ah, I'm so… That's exactly how I feel too.

Me: Actually, I broke up with Sam on Sunday.

Ty: Oh! Oh, wow, that's—

I could hear he was smiling. I was smiling too, ignoring the stomach ache I had from the images of Sam from Sunday swimming around me. I needed to change the subject.

Me: Hey, you know what? I was literally just working on Oli's question and I think I've got the answer.

Ty: No way! That's great! Can you come over now, actually? My parents won't be back for at least an hour.

I hung up and texted M to tell her what had happened before setting off. I think she was almost 95% as happy about this turn of events as I was.

When we got to Ty's we went straight to his bedroom. I had a sudden flashback to the last time I'd been there, which made my whole neck come up in goosebumps. Wow, I felt turned on. One look at Ty's face showed me that his thoughts were entirely on the computer rather than on what had happened last time we were on the bed, so I swallowed hard and tried to ignore the feeling of my stomach getting sucked away.

When the computer was ready, I entered my answer to the secret question. No matter how many times I'd done it by now, it always made my heart go crazy. There was no suspense this time though – we were back in Oli's email straight away.

I blinked. It looked completely different this time – every message had been read. There had also been lots of new emails in the last few days. Oli hadn't answered any of them though.

Ty scrolled down the page slowly. At first nothing looked interesting. There were a few enquiries from people who wanted Oli for a job. Oli hadn't cleaned up his inbox and there were also quite a few adverts and newsletter emails, which he'd just read and left there, without deleting them. But then we spotted it – one email *had* been answered since last time we'd looked. It was the one from Karim, telling Oli he'd tried tracking his phone. Oli had answered: *You know you can't catch me with your unsophisticated efforts. I'm just busy working on something, don't worry. Be back soon.*

'Great, he answered Karim but can't be bothered to write to me,' Ty said. He looked deflated.

Of course – he'd been hoping to get a message from Oli this whole time. I wanted to put my arms around him, but instead I tried to stay encouraging. 'Oli might write at any moment,' I suggested, 'or we might see a new important email come in now that we have access again.' I don't think any of it perked him up that much, though, and overall neither of us was in a very optimistic mood when I left not long after.

| 6 |

Liars and Truth-Tellers

This morning, as soon as Ty spotted me, he walked straight over. 'I can stay with you,' he offered. 'Or pretend we've never met – however you prefer to deal with the situation.'

Behind him, groups were congregating and whispers amplifying.

'I think I'm in the pretend-we've-never-met-camp. At least until half-term,' I muttered.

'Ok. Do you want me to do a secret signal occasionally so we're clear that I remember we have in fact met each other? You know, scratching my left eyebrow with my right index, that kind of thing. So we avoid any kind of misunderstanding like last time.'

'Ok, yeah. Umm, you could go like this with your right hand and this with your left hand, and then put them together like this,' I said, making a heart with my index fingers and thumbs.

'Fine, I get it, no secret sign,' he smiled.

'I'll be fine, honestly,' I said.

M appeared at my side. 'She'll be fine, I'll deflect the death stares.'

Ty gave her a faint smile. 'Thanks,' he said, and then to me: 'Can we talk after school?'

I nodded and he walked off. I linked arms with M, sighing, as we made our way to assembly. Only four more days before half-term.

Assembly was a demonstration of a new platform the school has bought to help us apply for university, called Unifrog. Much of the session was taken up by our IT team attempting to re-member how to log into the school's brand-new iPad. Everyone looked sick with uni application stress, but I sent my application out on time a few days ago, so I figured there was no point worrying about it now.

Me: At least that's one thing I don't have to stress out about. A welcome break from the whole rest of my life.

M: Yeah, I don't have to think about it either.

Me: What do you mean?

M: Oh, I sent my application out last week as well.

Me: Wait – what? You did what? You did something early? No way!

M: It's a ploy. That way, the unis will think I'm also applying to Oxbridge [she wiggled her eyebrows].

Me: That might be the most ridiculous thing I've ever heard... or it might be genius.

M: It's genius.

I looked across the room and spotted Ty. He was in the sick-with-stress camp.

Me: Hey. Do you think I should tell Ty about Sam?

M: Um, no?

Me: But isn't it bad karma to start off a relationship with such a big lie?

M: It's fine, you're offsetting that with all the good karma from helping with Oli. Overall, you're on the plus side.

Me: I'm being serious, M!

M: So am I! Why would you tell him? He told you he liked you when you still had a boyfriend. He should expect that access to your vagina – or, I guess, your mouth – wouldn't be exclusive right away.

Me: Thanks M, a bit graphic there.

M: You asked for my opinion.

Me: And I got it, yup, all of it. Didn't keep any of it to yourself.

M: You're welcome.

I smiled at her. I felt a bit less bad. M is the queen of justifying decisions after you've already made them. I mean, I'm still a cheater, but at least it officially counts as cheating on only one person, not two (yay?).

I think I would feel much better (as in, like a less-terrible human) if Sam was talking to me, but so far three calls and five very grovelling WhatsApp messages have not done the trick. I feel that those numbers are approaching harassment territory. He's also blocked me on all social media. I mean, he's not on TikTok, and his Instagram is all embarrassingly earnest filtered photos of countryside views and I never appreciated it at all when I had access to it, but its absence has made a far bigger hole in my life than I would have imagined. All I can do is look periodically at the still-grey WhatsApp ticks, willing them to turn blue.

After school, I found Ty outside and we walked away together quickly.

'What did you want to talk about?' I asked.

'The GCHQ guys came back last night,' he told me right away.

'Oh my god! Did they say more about what's going on?'

'They didn't tell me anything at all actually. They only talked to my parents, who made me stay in my room.' Ty looked annoyed. 'I asked them about it afterwards and they did answer most of my questions, but not everything. The GCHQ guys just said the same as last time – they're trying to locate Oli, but they didn't explain why. When I asked my parents what they thought it was about, they finally confirmed that I was I was right about "Hong Kong"' He made quote marks with fingers. 'Oli never went to Hong Kong. He'd hacked into something he shouldn't have, something really illegal, and he was hiding from cyber security agencies. My parents think he's done something like that again now.'

'What did he hack into back then?'

'That's the part my parents won't tell me,' Ty said moodily. 'They explained that at the time they'd had to fight really hard to keep his name out of the papers because they didn't want his future to be affected. He was a minor, so they were able to make sure it didn't happen. Now they say that there's no point bringing back the past. Almost no one knows, and they want to keep it that way. As if I'd tell anyone...'

'You'd tell me,' I pointed out.

'Well. Yes.' There was a faint smile on his lips. 'Are you saying my parents have a point?'

'I guess I am.' I smiled too. Isn't it the most annoying thing in the world when someone else tells you that your parents are right? 'This is all so crazy,' I said. 'I can't believe you're just learning about it now.'

'Yeah, I know. It's like... I don't know, honestly, like he was Batman all along or something.'

'So did you see the GCHQ guys yourself?' I asked. 'Was it the same ones as last time?

'I only saw one of them, and yes I recognised him from last time. At one point he left the living room where he was with my parents and his colleague – I guess he said he needed the loo, but he didn't go into the bathroom at all. I heard him go into Oli's room. He looked around for a couple of minutes and then he came into my room but I was in there so he couldn't do anything – just pretended he'd got the wrong door.'

I opened my eyes wide. 'Looking for clues?'

'Yeah,' Ty shrugged. 'Oli's note was in my pocket anyway. At least the situation was awkward enough for him that he couldn't really ask why I'd never passed on his card to my parents.'

'How did your parents take all of this?'

Ty sighed. 'Dad is in a terrible mood. He's angry at Oli for putting them through this again. Mum is more worried than angry. Oli isn't a minor anymore, so if he's done something... he might go to jail this time.'

'And you, what do you think?'

'I just... I thought that Oli was lying low, hiding from SPAM. But now he's answering his friend's email, and doing stuff that's got GCHQ looking for him?' He shrugged. 'I don't know what to think anymore.'

'Ty...' I said slowly. 'You know you can decide to tell your parents about everything. About the note, and what we've found out. I know Oli asked you not to, but he'd understand how worried you got. And your parents know some of the missing pieces, like what Oli did five years ago. Maybe they'd be able to put it all together.'

Ty was silent for a bit, biting his lip in the way I could watch for hours and hours. His voice had sounded almost a tiny bit cracked before and I wanted to hug him, but when he spoke again, he sounded calmer.

'Given what my parents were saying last night, I think they'd just tell GCHQ everything right away. I just want to find him first, Clara. Us, not... people who would arrest him.'

'Ok,' I said.

'We said half-term,' he reminded me.

'We did,' I agreed.

'I feel like we're so close. We have all the information, we just haven't connected it yet. It's like when I try to do a maths problem, to be honest.' He smiled unconvincingly.

We each went back to our own home. I was greeted by Emma's shrill voice from half a block away. *Great, just what I need*, I thought, *more of this*. I figured I'd eat whatever I found in the fridge straight from the Tupperware and then creep upstairs to hide like a reasonable person. Well, that is *not* how it ended up going down...

As I got closer, I could hear that tonight's row was about their *mums and daughters* ballet class, an embarrassing bonding exercise that Mum has recently instated: a group of 6–10 year-olds in tutus and leotards; a mix of exhausted and sprightly mothers in leggings aggressively eyeing each other to compare which one of their progeny is the most naturally talented; and then Emma, surly, refusing to do any of the steps properly, and Mum smiling too much and calling her 'sweetie' every two seconds in a passive-aggressive tone.

'I don't *want* to go anymore!' Emma screeched, with the manic intensity of someone who is several hours past her bedtime.

'But why, darling? You asked me to do this class! You begged! And it's so fun doing it together,' Mum answered in her faux-calm voice. That hair-raising tone only ever gets me more angry and it obviously had the same effect on Emma. She positively screamed.

'I don't want to do anything with you ever again!'

Ok. This wasn't just Emma's normal level of being annoying. She was all red like a little goblin, her body shaking with a fury that seemed too big for her. I stepped in.

'Hey, Emma, you're ok,' I said. 'Why don't you tell me what's wrong?'

Mum looked relieved that I'd appeared. I noticed that she was wearing a tracksuit which I didn't even know she owned, and her hair was unbrushed and maybe even dirty. (Wow, I turn my attention to something else for a couple of days and this family just disintegrates – everyone with the best timing, as always.)

Emma started crying, which only amplified when I put my arms around her. Mum made a movement as if to join the hug but I waved at her to stop. 'What is it?' I asked Emma. 'Just tell me, I promise you'll feel better. You can hardly feel worse than this, can you?'

Emma nodded wetly. 'I saw the messages,' she sniffled.

'You saw what messages?'

Behind her, I saw Mum's face suddenly drop.

'The messages on Mum's phone.'

Mum's face was positively ashen now.

'Whose messages? What did they say?' I asked.

'From *your* dad,' Emma said ferociously. 'They're *fucking!*' She was almost a little gleeful, correctly sensing that the gravity of the situation meant no one would pick up on her language.

'Whoa, whoa,' I said.

How did *Emma* know about this? She was so upset. I realised that in all my suppositions, I'd never seriously considered how she would feel about it – I'd thought of it as almost a bit funny. But now that I saw her scrunched-up little face, it made my heart break.

'Mum?' I said pointedly.

'It's complicated,' Mum said finally.

Emma and I rolled our eyes in unison.

'Don't worry, Emma,' I said flippantly, 'you don't need parents anyway. You can just come and live with me when I get my own place. I'll be out of here in a few months.'

Emma started to wail, and Mum shot me a dark look. 'Clara, you're really not helping. Anyway...' She sighed. 'Justin and I actually talked just a couple of days ago. We've ended it.'

'You've *ended* it? Ended *what*, exactly?'

'Nothing! It was nothing. It was... John and I are having a difficult time, and I just did something... Familiarity is comforting, that's all. I got carried away. It was a mistake, obviously. Emma, your dad and I are still very much together, and we are going to work this out, I promise.'

'But he's been sleeping on the sofa downstairs,' Emma whined.

My god, was there anything that girl didn't know? She's a regular spy – I had no idea John had been sleeping downstairs.

Mum sighed. 'How do you...? It's temporary, I promise.'

'How can you promise when you're not even *trying* to make it better?!' Emma pouted.

'Yes, and why *Dad* of all people?' I added. 'Couldn't you just have an affair with a random guy not related to your daughter, like a normal person? Never mind the option – sorry if this is a crazy thought – of not having affairs at all?'

Mum looked at the two of us glaring at her angrily and I saw her eyes fill with water. 'Girls, please,' she said. 'I understand that you're really upset, but I think we all need to calm down for now. There's no point talking in this state.'

'Ok, great,' I huffed, totally unmoved by her cracked voice. 'We need to *calm down* about you all deciding to turn our life into a soap opera, do we? Well, I guess I'm just going to go upstairs and *calm down*, then.'

'Oh Clara, come on,' Mum pleaded. 'I do want to talk this out, but you need to realise that you perhaps don't understand the situation fully.'

'What, I couldn't understand it because I'm not a *grown-up*? Is there something special that happens when you become a *grown-up* that makes it fine to cheat on people?'

Mum winced, and I stomped off to the stairs.

'I'm coming too,' Emma declared, and followed.

I flopped down on my bed, feeling horrible. Obviously, my outburst had been directed towards myself as much as Mum. I checked my WhatsApp messages to Sam. At some point the ticks had turned blue, but there was still no answer.

The entire house was quiet and dark. I imagined the three of us, Emma, Mum and me, lying awake in the dark, each in our separate bedrooms. It was very late and silent and John was still at work.

Wednesday 19th October

I woke up after a restless night, to a text from Ty. He wanted me to come and meet him in the library when I finished my classes, which was both mysterious and also not really in keeping with our plan to act like we had no wish to be in the same room as each other.

I made my way there in the afternoon. We were the only ones in the library, so that was one less stress at least. Ty was already sitting at one of the desks at the back when I walked in. He kissed me when I joined him, which immediately sparked images of us having sex against the *History – Middle Ages and Renaissance* shelf (the most sturdy, as I estimated from a quick look around).

I shook the thought out of my head and turned my attention back to what Ty was doing instead of the way his leg felt leaning against mine. He reached into his backpack and pulled out Oli's laptop. We both sat down at the desk.

'Last night I was trying to see if I could find any news about hacking or cyber crimes to figure out what Oli has been doing that's got GCHQ involved,' Ty told me. 'There was nothing that could see on the mainstream news, so I got into more specialised blogs, and Reddit and the SPAM public statements, etc. I didn't find what I was looking for, but I did stumble on something we hadn't seen before. There's, like, a whole community of people who are obsessed with Spencer Ambrose, who think he's some sort of hero. They all dream about being invited to join SPAM, and they run elaborate hacks just in the hope that he'll notice them and get in touch. There's even a subreddit about it, where people exchange tips on the sort of thing that they think Spencer finds impressive. And look – I found this thread of people discussing a mysterious website they think was set up by Spencer.'

Ty turned the computer so I could see. He was on the URL www.hkzn.com. The site was blank, with just a button that said *enter.*

'Why do they think it's been set up by Spencer?'

'HKZN is sort of the mirror-image of SPAM. S is the 19th letter from the start, H is the 19th letter from the end, P is the 16th letter from the start, K is the 16th letter from the end, etc. And also...'

He highlighted the top-right corner, which had looked simply black. But when it was highlighted, that spiral shape from the email showed up again – the Fibonacci spiral. *I forgot to look that up*, I thought to myself.

'It's not very sophisticated,' Ty shrugged, 'but it's there. I haven't pressed *enter* yet, because the people on the thread say you can only try once. They say that when you click the button, you have to solve a problem before a timer runs out.'

'What happens after you solve it?'

'Well, if you get it wrong or don't do it in time, you get locked out forever. Then some people on the thread say that they got it right, and they were sent a second, harder problem by an anonymous person, and then nothing else ever happened.'

He pointed to a line on the screen:

FUZuck: it's been 2 mths now, think it's dead for me?

QuantumFr0g: I heard that if you're in you know within the day

FUZuck: damn. good luck everyone

FremenO: Don't listen to someone who says he 'herd something' – he knows nothing

FUZuck: so u think there's still a chance?

'I looked at quite a lot of the thread,' Ty told me, 'and no one seems to have got past that second-question stage, but there are two people who were involved in the discussion early on and they said they had got through the first stage. They never came back to discuss what happened after and so people are speculating that they got in, or got through to a later stage at least, and they're not allowed to talk about it.'

'So this HKZN is a sort of recruiting website?'

'Yes. Of course, it could have nothing to do with Spencer,' Ty said. 'Actually, some people on the thread think that it's someone else entirely, another person who's just trying to get Spencer's attention by running an elaborate type of scam. But...' He trailed off.

I looked at him. 'So, I guess that you want me to try the problem that comes up on the website? Ty, I've never had to do anything with a timer before. I have to research everything for days.'

'I know.'

'And even if I get it right, who knows what would happen with the second problem.'

'Yes, I know, Clara. But after the first one, they'd get in contact with us,' Ty said. 'And maybe that would lead to another clue.' He looked straight into my eyes. 'It's the only thing we've got right now.'

I sighed. 'I just don't want you to get your hopes up too much.'

'I won't. I'm not. No hoping here,' Ty said, looking really very hopeful.

I sighed again. I mean – obviously I would never have said no. But there was almost no chance I'd get the answer and Ty would end up more disappointed than before – I was really not looking forward to watching his face when it happened. 'Ok. I'll try,' I said.

'Yes! Thank you.' He kissed me quickly, a hot, excited kiss, which made this seem very worth it for a second at least. 'Thank you!' He looked at the time. 'There's thirty-five minutes left until my next period, and apparently the timer is never more than just a few minutes. Want to do it now?'

'Yeah, ok.' I took a deep breath and clicked the *enter* button. A question came up, with a box at the bottom for an answer. A timer started counting down seconds from five minutes in the top right corner of the screen. The question had a lot of words and I was so nervous that everything swam in front of my eyes and I thought I'd forgotten how to read. I closed my eyes, counted to three, and opened them again. This time, at least, the words stayed in place:

Question: You are lost in the desert, and you come to a crossroads. You know that one of the roads leads

---

you to the town where you can get water and food, and the other one leads you deeper into the desert, where you will die a horrible death.

There are no signs telling you which road is which, but there are two people standing at the crossroads. They only answer yes/no questions.

You have been told that one of them always tells the truth, and the other one always lies, but they are twins and you can't tell who is who. You are only allowed to ask one question. How can you find out if you should take the road on the left or the road on the right to survive?

'It's a logic problem!' I exclaimed.

'What?'

'This question – you don't need to know any advanced maths to do it. It's just a logic problem – I really like them.'

A flicker of hope appeared in Ty's eyes and suddenly I felt very nervous that I was overpromising. I do really like logic problems though. Like, who should sit next to who at dinner if Jess hates David and Kendra loves Nicole. I like turning them round and round in my head until everything just fits.

I put my head in my hands and started thinking, but Ty kept fidgeting and distracting me, so I asked him to go somewhere else. He wandered away and I could hear him taking books off the shelves and putting them back in with a *clack*, but it was still better than having him in front of me. I got to work.

I started imagining myself at that crossroads. Obviously, you can't just walk up to one of the twins and say, 'Will the road on the right lead me to safety?' because you don't know whether you're talking to the liar or not. And if you try to ascertain which one is the liar (by asking for example something like, 'Is the desert hot?' to see if they answer the truth) then you've used up your only question. What you need is a question that will manage to encompass both the liar/not liar part and the road part. But you can't ask 'Is the desert hot and will the road on the right lead me to safety?' because that's two questions. So how can you get both things into just one question?

I think the adrenaline must have been pushing me along because I got a sudden brainwave: you don't actually need to know *which* twin is a liar and which one isn't. The only thing you need is to find a question that they would *both answer the same*, so that it doesn't matter which one you've asked. They answer the opposite of each other when asked a straight question – so you need to find a question that encompasses both of their answers in one go.

I was getting that hot-brain feeling when I know I'm on the point of cracking a problem. That was it! I had to ask one twin about what the other twin would say: if I asked the truth-teller about what the liar would say, he'd say the truth about a lie – which is a lie – and if I asked the liar about what the truth-teller would say, he'd say a lie about the truth – which is also a lie. I'd always get a lie! It's like multiplying numbers: if the liar is negative and the truth-teller positive, + times – is the same as – times +: it's always – !

I wrote down my idea slowly: go up to one of them and ask, 'Would your twin tell me that the road on the right is the one leading to safety?'

Then I drew up a little table to verify what answer I would get, for all the possible options:

	Road on the right leads to safety	Road on the right leads to desert
Liar says:	No	Yes
Truth-teller says:	No	Yes

It worked! You'd always get a lie as the answer, so if the answer was no, you should take the road on the right, and if the answer was yes, you should take the one on the left.

'I think I've got it!' I shouted to the room.

Ty rushed over. There were twenty-seven seconds left on the timer. I typed in the answer, read it over quickly for typos (of which there were several because of the annoying sticky A key) and entered it with three seconds left. The whole screen went black, and a box asking for an email address appeared.

'Put yours in,' Ty said. 'So it's not the same last name as Oli.'

I entered my email, and the page went completely blank. Refreshing it changed nothing.

'That's it?' I asked.

'Yeah. You don't know if anything will happen until it does.' Ty shrugged.

I couldn't help looking all around the room. It felt like someone somewhere was watching us and discussing my performance.

'Hey,' Ty said with a proud smile. 'You did it!'

'Yeah.'

'So stop thinking about it now.'

He looked pleased and confident, but I couldn't relax. I kept second-guessing myself, wondering whether maybe I'd forgotten to think about something in the question, wondering if, or when, the next message would come.

'I can't stop,' I said.

Ty cupped my face with both his hands. 'Does this help?' He kissed me.

It did. 'It does,' I said in a small voice.

Ty smiled. He looked back to the computer and clicked on the tab with the Reddit thread again. He refreshed the page to see if there were any new messages and started scrolling down. There were a lot of people talking on the thread, dozens of them, but a few of the usernames came back more than the others.

Suddenly, Ty started. 'Clara,' he said, 'look at this one.' He pointed to one of the lines I'd read before:

FremenO: Don't listen to someone who says he 'herd something' – he knows nothing

'The *a* is missing,' I said, suddenly realising what he was thinking.

Ty scrolled down more, looking for another message from the same poster. 'Here,' he whispered when he found one.

FremenO: It's a faake, trust me

'A double *a*,' I said.

'Like when you're pressing too hard on a sticky key,' Ty said, lightly tapping the A key on the laptop which had been giving me trouble earlier.

'And the username...'

'Yeah,' Ty said. 'Fremen are the desert people in *Dune*. And the O... for Fremen Oli.'

I bit my lip. 'So you think it's him?'

Ty didn't answer. He scrolled down a bit more, until he hit another message from FremenO.

> **FremenO:** HKZN is a faake, I'm sure of it. The only waay to get Spencer's attention is if you do something really wesome. Then he'll come and find you.
>
> **4RCH4NG3L:** Ok genius, how come he hasn't come to find you yet?
>
> **FremenO:** Working on it ;)

Ty looked at me. 'So he *was* trying to join them,' he said softly. 'I was totally wrong.'

In just a few minutes Ty had gone from the most hopeful I'd seen him to completely dejected. I didn't know what to say. I put my hand on his arm and left it there – I wasn't even sure if he was feeling it.

In this funk, I stomped over to Dad's. I did not feel like dealing with Mum again. She had a whole husband and second child to keep her company, but Dad would be on his own. A breakup couldn't be easy at any age, especially not when you're dealing with someone you used to be crazy in love with – and after eight years working super hard, in relationship limbo. I looked forward to giving him a hug.

Dad was in the kitchen when I arrived, making a pie. He looked surprised. 'Clara! Was I expecting you?'

'No,' I said.

I waited, but he just kept rolling out his crust and making elaborate decorative patterns.

'I know about you and Mum,' I added finally.

'Oh. Right. She told me.'

'So?'

He put his knife down and looked at me. 'I'm not sure what you want me to say, Clara.'

'I mean… just say *something*, let's start with that!'

'It happened, it's over. There's nothing to say.'

'How can there be nothing to say?!' I shouted. 'This is *Mum* we're talking about. It's not like some fling with a random woman! You guys are my *parents!*'

Dad crossed his arms. 'I'm not going to have this conversation with you, Clara. This is my private life. If your mother wants to talk to you about it that's her prerogative, but I like my privacy. So we can have some civilised conversation, or we can just not talk, your choice.' He went back to his pie, a bit shakily.

'*Civilised conversation!* Aaargh!' I huffed. 'I'm going to my room!' I clambered up the stairs.

'The pie will be ready in an hour!' Dad called after me.

I slammed my door shut and flung myself on the bed. What is wrong with the two of them?! Someone please explain how I'm supposed to learn open and honest communication with role models like these. The previous generation are seriously messed up!

| 7 |

The One-Time Pad Code

When I woke up this morning, my first thought went to Ty. He was so upset and dejected yesterday. He said that we should just stop looking for Oli and let whatever happened happen. I wondered if he was now going to show his parents Oli's note and tell them about what we'd been doing, but I didn't say a word about it because Ty's mood seemed too precarious to handle any kind of additional moral questioning.

I searched my brain for a realisation that would explain away everything that we'd learned, but there was nothing. I mean, the puzzle all fit together perfectly: Oli had joined SPAM, and now he was running a hacking job with them – and they had caught the attention of GCHQ, who were now looking for him. Though what exactly had Oli done? That still bothered me. I looked at the news again, but there was absolutely no cyber-crime news.

It was like every single hacker in the world had decided to take a holiday.

It was another not-so-fun day at school in the Alice department. M has taken to walking in between me and any hostile glares as if she's some sort of human shield, but this doesn't feel very sustainable.

At least I have my parents' drama to distract myself. M has remained, of course, extremely invested in the whole debacle. She'd been upset to hear about the spectacular way her fairy-tale dream had been dashed the other day, and today she was very worried about the ill effects that bottling up all his feelings would have on my dad's long-term health prospects.

It was a toss-up who I would find the least annoying out of the two of them, but after school I decided to go to back to Mum's for some variation in (dis)pleasures. She was there already when I came in, with John and Emma too.

Wow, John looked rough. I realised that I hadn't seen him for a few days and the sofa was clearly not agreeing with him. And his work disaster showed no sign of being fixed. 'Money is still disappearing from random accounts,' he told us, looking like he'd had all the life zested out of him.

'Shall we have dinner all together?' Mum asked a bit warily.

I nodded.

'Can we order pizza?' Emma piped up.

There were more enthusiastic nods all around this time.

Dinner was actually extremely nice. We put everything on pause for a bit. Emma was chatty and sweet, Mum was nervous and smiley and John seemed genuinely happy to be by her side. How could I have never noticed the way he looked at her before, like she was made out of precious stones – or made out of piles of bank notes or whatever people like him get moony-eyed over?

After dinner, John went back to his office and Emma pulled the child card and left Mum and me to clear the table.

'Darling,' she said, as we were stacking plates in the dishwasher in perfect domestic union, 'I understand that you want to talk about it. I really do want you to feel like you can ask me anything, and I'm sorry that I made it feel like this wasn't the case. It just that, well… sometimes life is messier than you can see from where you are. It's not all as perfect as you and Sam.'

My heart dropped all the way into my feet. I suddenly missed Sam violently. How absolutely unthinkable that he had no idea what was going on with my family. He *was* my family. He knew them all almost as well as I did. He'd want to know about all this. He *should* know about all this. I could feel tears flooding my eyes.

Mum put the fork she was holding down on the counter. 'Sweetheart... oh, I didn't realise that—'

'It's not that,' I said. 'It's Sam. He hates me.'

'Oh, darling. Do you want to tell me what happened?'

'I broke up with him,' I explained euphemistically, with a sniffle.

'I see... Is it – you don't have to tell me, but – is it that boy you mention a lot from your class? Ty?'

I eyed her suspiciously. Was she a mind reader? I swear I hadn't mentioned Ty *a lot*. Not any more than I mentioned, I don't know... ok fine, maybe I did mention him lots.

I nodded wetly.

Mum put a hand on my arm. 'Well, I don't know exactly what happened, of course, but one thing I can tell you for sure is that Sam doesn't hate you. He'll never hate you.'

'You really think that? He's not answering any of my calls or messages.'

'That's not hate. That's hurt. Sam is a very sensitive boy,' she added wistfully. I knew she would take this one hard.

She took the plate from my hands. 'I can finish up here,' she said. 'You just go and do something nice.'

I climbed up the stairs to my room. For the millionth time, I scrolled through my camera roll until I found Sam's goofy face. *I miss you, I miss you*, I wanted to shout at him. I started typing the words, but it felt like quite a scumbag move to make this all about me, so I did nothing.

Suddenly I remembered the application Sam had sent me to look at. I put my face in my hands. I'd never read it in the end. I kept forgetting, and Sam never reminded me because... well, because he's Sam and much too nice. *He's obviously way better off without me*, I thought. It didn't make me feel any better.

I opened Sam's application and read it through. It was so good. He's going to be such a great teacher. My eyes were getting prickly again and I sighed. I sure seem to have an impressive capacity for wallowing.

I closed my eyes and forced my thoughts away from Sam. They wandered to Oli – I wished we knew what he'd done that had got GCHQ's attention. That way we'd at least know what Oli risked if he got caught.

When I opened my eyes again, they fell back on Sam's application. Suddenly I got a feeling like there was a word on the tip of my tongue. It had somehow been caused by something Sam had written. I read the application through again carefully. In one question, Sam talked about how easy it was to miss things that are right in front of you. He meant his realisation that he wanted to be a teacher, but the phrase scratched inside my head. I put my fingers on my temples. There was a thought in there somewhere, I just had to convince it to come out.

Then I stood straight up in my bed. John's bank – it had just been hacked! How could I not have made the connection before! Sam was right – talk about missing the thing right in your home! The hack hadn't made the news yet, but that was only because they'd been using all their connections to keep the story quiet while they tried to fix it from the inside. From what John said, the story was a big deal. A really big deal.

I got my computer out and googled the bank, plus *security breach*, thinking that perhaps a more specific search would lead to some small, specialised outlet who was already reporting the story. But instead, the page was flooded with stories from five years ago. I felt my whole body humming. Five years ago – that was when Oli had pretended to be in Hong Kong!

I clicked on one of the articles. The hacker wasn't named, but the article specified that it was a minor. The hacker had published the names and bank balances of a few well-known people, along with information about some carefully chosen transactions. There were names I recognised in there – ministers who'd had to resign. I actually vaguely remembered the story. I'd only been twelve when it had broken, but it had sparked a big tax-evasion scandal. A lot of powerful people had been caught out.

And this whole time, it had been Oli. Well, if I was right. But I must be right – the same bank had been hacked after a five-year interval! There was no way this was a coincidence.

I lay back down in bed and turned it round in my head some more. I thought about what Ty had told me about his brother. It was so crazy to think I hadn't met Oli. He'd been such a huge part of my life and my thoughts recently, I felt like I knew him. And something here... something didn't feel right.

Friday 21st October

Another horrid day at school, rendered a lot less horrid by the fact that it's the last one for ten days! What a relief. Let's hope that everyone forgets about my love life as swiftly as big companies forget their carbon pledges.

I didn't tell Ty about my realisation from last night because he was still looking extremely upset and I wasn't sure he could handle talking about Oli just yet. Besides, I had a niggling thought that I wanted to discuss with M. I counted down the minutes until lunchtime when I could fill her in on everything.

'Wow,' she said, 'Ty's already been walking around looking like England lost another match on penalties. How are you going to announce to him that his brother is stealing millions from people's bank accounts for this hacker overlord?' She squinted. 'Wait a minute. You've got a *thought*, haven't you?'

I laughed. 'How can you tell?!'

'Your got-a-thought forehead vein has come out.'

I rubbed my forehead with one finger.

'Yeah,' M added. 'Don't ever play poker. So, what's the thought?'

'Well,' I said. 'Stay with me on this, ok? I promise it's leading somewhere.'

'Ok. Go.'

'All right,' I said. 'Five years ago, Oli hacked into John's bank and exposed fraud and corruption among powerful people. Now, he hacks into the same bank again, but this time, he does what... just steals money?'

'Yeah,' M frowned. 'It's pretty different. Like, morally.'

'Add to that,' I continued excitedly, 'the fact that Oli hasn't been answering his messages. Five years ago, when he was hiding from cyber security agencies, he still somehow stayed in touch with his parents and with Ty. But this time, nothing.'

'But you said that he'd answered—'

'Aha!' I interrupted. 'Exactly, Karim's email! So, Oli doesn't check his emails for days, and when he finally reads them, he doesn't delete any of the adverts and spam (which he usually does), and he doesn't write to his family or give updates to people who are waiting on him for work. The only thing he does is answer Karim. That's really strange behaviour, isn't it?' I asked rhetorically. 'What's special about Karim's message? There were several other people asking Oli where he was, and he didn't bother answering those. But Karim's message *was* different. He wasn't just asking, he was actually looking for Oli. He'd even already found something out.'

'Ok… is this the part where you're supposed to be getting at something? Cause I'm not seeing it.'

I looked at her. 'I think that Oli isn't working *with* SPAM… they're somehow *making* him do it!' I said triumphantly. 'They found out that he was the one who'd hacked the bank five years ago, and they wanted him to do it again. Actually, one of the articles mentioned that in order to avoid jail time back then, he'd had to help the bank improve their security system, so he'd have really good knowledge of it. And we know that Spencer has blackmailed people into doing work for him before. What if that's what's happening with Oli? He probably doesn't have access to his messages at all. That might even be why we got locked out of his email – maybe they were locking Oli himself out on his own computer.'

'So you think it's Spencer who answered Karim's email, not Oli? So that Karim would stop looking for him?'

'Exactly,' I said. 'They're gaining time: I know from John that the attack on the bank is still ongoing. Maybe they're worried that Karim might get to Oli before they're done. I mean, he has – you know – technological know-how. Unlike us.'

M looked at me and put her chin in her hands.

'Very convincing, Sherlock,' she said. 'Except that Oli was *trying* to join SPAM. That's what he said on the forum Ty found.'

'Yeah. I don't know how that fits in,' I admitted. 'But come on, don't you think that SPAM controlling Oli is the only way to explain what's going on?'

'I don't know,' M waved her hands in the air. 'Maybe his personality has changed in the last five years. Not everyone stays an anti-capitalist warrior forever.'

'I mean, Ty told me that one of his latest personal projects was hacking into some Tory MP's Word software and making it type *TAX THE RICH* every time they tried to type *the*.'

She laughed. 'Fine. You've convinced me.'

'Oh good,' I said. 'I was trying it out on you first before I tell Ty what I'm thinking. In case you thought it was totally off and not worth confusing everything even more.'

'I think you can tell him, at least see what he thinks,' she declared. 'Wait—'

'What?'

'Maybe you can make even more sure.'

'How would I do that?' I asked.

'Well...' she squinted. 'What if you write Oli a message that's worrying enough for Spencer that he has to answer it? And you include something that only Oli could understand.'

'So if the person who replies doesn't get it, we'd know they're definitely not Oli...'

'Yeah, exactly. Do you know anything we could use? Like some secret between Ty and his brother?'

'I don't know,' I said slowly, trying to remember all the things Ty had told me. 'They have a joke about what book Oli's name is from. If it's *Oliver Twist* vs *Lady Chatterley* – Oli claims the latter.'

'Ok, I can work with that,' M said. 'Give me your phone.'

I handed it to her. 'Write it from your own email,' I instructed, 'in case they recognise mine from when I did the problem on that weird website. And also, please think about what you write very carefully.'

She had that excited look in her eyes, and M's impulse control isn't the best.

'I know,' she brushed me off. 'It has to be enough pressure to get them to answer, but not so much that they freak out and, like... make anyone *disappear*.'

I pursed my lips at her. 'Yes, M, it would be better to avoid that.'

'What?' She shrugged at me. 'Just making it clear that I understand the gravity of my role. But fear not, I am a master of the finely-crafted word.'

I watched as she typed, deep in concentration.

She looked up. 'How's this?' she suggested. 'Hey Oliver Twist, just bumped into Karim. He was worried about you – said you brushed him off a few days ago. Thought I'd check in before he starts a full-on manhunt, how are you?'

'Ah,' I approved. 'Good angle talking about Karim. Send it.'

She clicked send and handed the phone back to me.

'I hope you're right, that he's not working with SPAM,' she said thoughtfully. 'They sound awful.'

'Lots of people want to work with Spencer,' I pointed out. 'We saw on the forum – they think he's the best hacker that's ever lived. And that he's an anarchist hero who goes against everyone – rich, poor, famous, unknown...'

'That's it though,' M said. 'When you don't take sides, you're taking a side.'

'Yeah, you're right,' I agreed. 'I was looking into it more and – all the rich, powerful people that SPAM have gone after over the years... nothing's really changed for them. Not long-term, anyway. They still have money, they still have important jobs, comfortable lives. Sure, they might have had to resign when a scandal first struck, but within months it was all brushed under the carpet. But a few years ago SPAM went after a charity – I don't know if you remember this from the news? It was a medium-sized charity that fought against childhood hunger in the UK. SPAM exposed the fact that the director had done deals with huge agribusiness compagnies that were exploiting workers in Asia and Africa, even though he claimed the food was all produced locally in the UK. The charity had to fold after SPAM exposed them. They were feeding two thousand children a year, and now no one's taking care of those children anymore. The agribusiness companies are still going, of course.'

'That's what I'm saying,' M shrugged pointedly.

I hoped that John would be around again when I got home so that I could get more information from him about what was happening at the bank, but he was at work, and he's still there now at 11pm. I guess that one day of coming home at normal-human hours was all he could spare in the crisis.

Then M texted me: *Just got an answer. Oli blowing me off, making a point of telling me to pass on to Karim that everything is fine. Didn't pick up on the Oliver Twist thing at all.*

I told her to answer, making it sound like she believed him. Did I have enough of a case to call Ty now? I turned it round in my head, and finally I picked up my phone.

When he answered, I took a deep breath, getting prepared to explain my whole thought process to him. But in the end, I didn't have to. He'd been thinking about Oli's email to Karim as well.

'*Unsophisticated effort?*' Ty repeated. 'Oli would never use those words. But you know who has?'

'Spencer Ambrose,' I remembered suddenly.

'Yup. In his statement—'

'About the Casino job in Nevada. Oh my god.'

I let myself fall down on my bed. SPAM have Oli – and they're somehow forcing him to work for them.

Saturday 22nd October

I woke up to muffled voices downstairs. I looked at the time. I realised Mum and Emma were out and it was just John downstairs, talking on the phone. *He must be working from home,* I thought. We were on our own – perfect.

I quickly pulled on some clothes and went downstairs. John was on his phone in the kitchen, putting together a sad bowl of All-Bran cereal. He looked at me warily. We were in a truce, but I guess he didn't fully trust that I'd waved the white flag. I smiled sweetly (I hoped) and started putting my own breakfast together. I didn't want to stress him out by just standing around.

He said goodbye to the person he was talking to and gestured to the kitchen table, as I'd hoped he would. We sat across from each other. It was... more than a little weird. I'd spent eight years of my life avoiding this situation at all costs, and my body was fully in *just leave now* mode.

I looked at him, crunching his cereal, looking tense, and I realised that he was feeling the exact same way. The realisation struck me as so hilarious, I just couldn't help it – I started giggling uncontrollably and soon I was really laughing. At first John looked at me, astonished, but pretty soon he'd joined in. When we managed to catch our breath, John looked a lot more relaxed.

'Well, this is new,' he said.

'We're trying it out,' I said.

'It's all right so far.'

I smiled. 'Better than dealing with work?' (Please admire my smooth transition.)

John sighed. 'A lot better,' he said. 'That was the *Daily Mail*. They want to run the story tomorrow. I think we've stalled them as much as we can, they'll print what they want now.'

'What is the story exactly?'

'Well...' John frowned. 'I'm not completely sure, actually. At first it seemed like a straightforward hacking job; a pretty sophisticated, one – sophisticated enough that our cyber-security team still hasn't managed to stop it – but still, straightforward.'

'But now it's not so straightforward?'

'No. It's really very strange...'

John eyed me appraisingly.

'I won't tell anyone,' I said quickly.

He sighed again. 'It'll be all over the news soon anyway, I guess,' he said. 'Well, the first few days, as I was saying, they did the expected: took money out of some accounts. It was just small amounts, but very fast, from thousands of different accounts, piling up quickly. They seem to know exactly how our security systems operate and how we were going to keep changing them to try to stop the attack. Every change we made, they just changed with us.'

'Is it really a lot of money?' I asked.

'Yes. Really a lot,' he confirmed.

Wow, when a banker says lots of money, it must be... really *really* lots of money. Like, private-island amounts of money.

'What will happen if you can't get the money back?' I asked.

'We're...' he looked sideways at me. 'We're talking to the government about a bailout.'

'Oh,' I said.

'Yeah,' he said.

He was obviously waiting for me to have opinions about this, which I very much did, but I swallowed them and smiled at him, to his evident relief. I had a mystery to solve, so reform-a-banker day would have to wait. 'What's made it not straightforward?' I prompted.

'Well,' John went on, 'we started noticing something new. Occasionally, instead of taking money out, they were putting money *into* the bank accounts.'

'What? That's so weird.'

'Yes. They've only done it a handful of times and it's much, much less than they take out, so overall they are still hugely making money, but it doesn't make any sense.'

My mind was racing.

'What would they be doing that for?'

'We can't figure it out. It's almost like they're just playing games with us at this point. And they're winning.' He frowned. 'We can't stop the money from coming in any more than we've managed to stop it going out. The really weird thing is that they're not doing it in pounds. They're adding in the exact same amount, every single time, but in Omani Rial. Why Omani Rial? They don't seem to be based there or anything.'

His phone pinged, and he looked at it.

'It's just happened again! Look.'

He turned his phone screen towards me. '*OMR 82436.52,*' I read. I almost stopped breathing. *OMR* – Oliver Manesh Rai.

I stuffed my remaining toast in my face as fast as I could and rushed upstairs to call Ty. He answered on the first ring.

Ty: Hello?

Me: Ty – I think Oli is sending us a message!

Ty: Wait, you think what? You got a message from him?

Me: Not exactly. I was just talking to John about what is happening at his bank. And listen to this. The hacker was just taking money at first, but now, he is doing a weird thing putting money *into* bank accounts. And it's not in pounds, it's in Omani Rial. And the code for Omani Rial is... OMR!

Ty: Oh my g—

Me: I know!

Ty: But – why would Oli send his message in such an obscure way? He can't know that you're connected to John.

Me: I wondered that too, but the story is about to be all over the news. John said it's going to be in the papers tomorrow. So it's not actually obscure – we're just a bit ahead.

Ty: So you think Ty expects us to see the message along with everyone else when it gets printed tomorrow? If that's the case, then this is amazing luck! It means SPAM can't be aware that we know anything about it yet!

Me: I know. If we can figure it out today, maybe we could catch them unawares.

Ty: Figure it out? What's the message?

Me: Well, I'm not sure. He keeps transferring the same amount of money into different accounts, but the number itself doesn't mean anything to me. Do you have something to write it down?

Ty: Wait. I'm outside. I was just playing football [I heard scratching noises as he put his phone down and picked it up again] Ok. I'm ready.

Me: It's 82436.52.

Ty: [a pause] No, it doesn't mean anything to me either.

Me: If Oli was trying to communicate with you, what code do you think he would use?

Ty: I think... Well, I think he'd use a one-time pad code. The one I told you about before – his favourite one. But you need a one-time pad for that.

Me: What's a one-time pad exactly?

Ty: It's a piece of paper that you have to keep secret, and it has a random list of letters on it, which make the key. You're supposed to use it only once and then you throw it away. If you do that, then the code is unbreakable. If you reuse the same one you make it less secure.

Me: Ok. Did Oli leave you a piece of paper with letters on it before he left? Or is there somewhere he could have hidden one?

Ty: Hmm... I definitely haven't seen one anywhere. I guess he could have hidden it when he came over to leave me the note—

Both: —*the note!*

Ty: It has those random capital letters. I always thought that was weird. I mean, Oli isn't a literary mastermind, but he still knows how capitalisation works. So maybe they make the key! [I heard more rustling as he retrieved the note from his pocket] Ok, so the capital letters are T, A, T, M, S, W.

Me: What do you do next? To decode the message?

Ty: You… Wow, this is all from a long time ago! Let me see. First of all, the key has to be the same length or longer than the message. And right now our key has six letters and our message has seven digits.

Me: Ok. So two of those digits at least must go together to make a two-digit number. That way we're left with six numbers or fewer, for a six-letter key.

Ty: That would work. All the numbers have to be 26 or less though, because they correspond to letters in the alphabet. Or, normally they do. Because normally you start from letters and turn them into numbers as the first step. But here we've got numbers already. So I don't know.

Me: I think that still makes sense. It's like Oli has done the first step for us. So we should still make sure the numbers are 26 or less.

I looked at the digits: 82436.52. The decimal point obviously meant nothing, so the digits we were working with, in order, were 8, 2, 4, 3, 6, 5, 2. I stared at them closely, trying to put them in pairs that were less than 27.

Me: There's only one possibility. The 2 and the 4 have to go together to make 24. Any other pair we try to make is more than 26.

Ty: Ok. So our coded message is 8, 24, 3, 6, 5, 2 and our key is T, A, T, M, S, W. We have to count the position of every letter for the key as well, so that's 20, 1, 20, 13, 19, 23.

Me: And then?

Ty: Then... Then you take away the key from the coded message. Or is it the other way round...? No, I'm pretty sure that's right. You take away the key from the coded message, number by number.

I wrote it down and read out my result to Ty:

$$\begin{array}{r} 8\ ,\ 24,\ \ 3\ ,\ 6\ ,\ \ 5,\ \ \ 2 \\ -\ \underline{20,\ \ 1\ ,\ 20,13,\ 19,\ 23} \\ -12\ ,\ 23\ ,\ -17,\ -7\ ,\ -14\ ,\ -21 \end{array}$$

Me: Most of them are negative numbers. What does that mean?

Ty: I remember that part. You have to add 26 to all the negative ones so they're positive again.

Me: Oh, so you're doing mod 26.

Ty: [laughing] Umm... I have no idea what that means, but I do remember Oli saying it too, so it must be right.

Me: Mod 26 means that you live in a world where there are only 26 numbers, 0 through 25. When you go past 25, you start again at 0, so 26 is 0, 27 is 1, 28 is 2, 29 is 3, and so on. And you can go the other way too, in the negative numbers: -1 is 25, -2 is 24, etc.

Ty: Right. I won't ask why we'd ever need to live in the world of 26 numbers. What message do we get mod 26?

I added the numbers in my head.

Me: We get 14, 23, 9, 19, 12, 5. Now we put that back into letters?

Ty: Yes. Just by doing 1 = A, 2 = B etc.

I counted on my fingers. I could hear Ty doing the same on the phone. *NWISLE.* My shoulders slumped. That couldn't be right, it didn't mean anything.

Me: What did you get?

Ty: Nwisle.

Me: Does *that* mean anything to you?

Ty: Nothing.

Me: Maybe we need to use a second code on it?

Ty: It does remind me of something...

I felt very frustrated all of a sudden. I wanted to crumple up my piece of paper and throw it against the wall. It's so much worse when you think you've got something and it turns out you haven't. I tried to think of more ideas.

Me: Maybe we could have used numbers that are more than 26, since we didn't start from letters. But then, there would have been so many possibilities, I don't understand how we could have got the right one... Or maybe the note wasn't the one-time pad after all. Or maybe it wasn't a one-time pad code at all.

Or maybe I've completely made up this whole idea, I thought crankily. I was quickly spinning down a spiral of despair.

Ty: Oh!

Me: What happened?

Ty: Nothing – I mean, I think I've got it!

Me: You figured out the right code?

Ty: No. I mean, yes – I think that we did everything correctly, and what we've got is a postcode!

Me: Oh my god! You're totally right!

Looking at the word again now, it seemed completely obvious. All of us live in the NW postcodes – those two letters will go together in my brain forever. Before Ty said it though, I would never have realised it myself.

Ty: Well, I guess sometimes being bad at maths makes your brain clearer, huh?

Me: Yeah. What a relief that you're so bad at maths, it's been a real help all this time.

Ty: Oh. Ha. Ha.

Me: [giggling] So this postcode – the space is in the middle, and the I must be a 1 and the S must be a 5, so we get NW1 5LE.

I typed it into Google Maps.

Ty: [whispering] It's so close to here!

He'd been doing the same thing. I stared at the pin on the map. It was about fifteen minutes from my house, probably less than ten minutes from Ty's.

Ty: Do you think he's telling us where he is?

Me: [whispering too] He has to be.

Ty: Ok. I guess I'll go tell my parents now and we'll call GCHQ together.

Me: Yeah.

Ty: ...

Me: Ty...

Ty: Clara...

Me: Don't say it—

Ty: —I think we should go check it out.

Me: Ty, come on! We agreed half-term, and it's half-term now.

Ty: It's not *actually* half-term. This is just the normal weekend, half-term doesn't start until Monday.

Me: That's so convoluted I'm actually impressed. It sounds like something M could have come up with.

Ty: [laughing] Come on. Don't you want to go too?

Me: Yes, of course I do. I just think that, you know, GCHQ are better-equipped to deal with scary hacking groups than I am.

Ty: But we still don't really know what's happening – I mean, what actually happened with SPAM, why Oli is sending this message, or if we're maybe going crazy and have invented the whole thing... Let's go just to see if we can make sure that we got the story right, at least.

Me: [suspiciously] Ok. To make sure.

Ty: [he cheered] Yes! Ok, can you give me one hour? I need to drop all this stuff off and get ready. Come meet me at home?

I hung up, extremely nervous and excited, and wrote this all down to make the hour pass before we actually go (!!)

| 8 |

Fibonacci Numbers

Saturday 22nd October – afternoon

Well, future reader, finally you are getting what you were promised – mystery, intrigue and action! I mean, this is still my life, so you'll have to wade through some awkward situations first, but we'll get there, I promise.

So here we go: after writing the last entry I got ready quickly before heading over to Ty's. Choosing an outfit was a bit of a quandary, but in the end I decided that my sweatpants, a sports bra I found at the back of the drawer and a long-sleeve top should cover a number of possible activities such as waiting for hours in a bush, or running away from bad guys without getting snagged on branches, or staying comfortable while being kidnapped.

I took the bus to Ty's, my heart thumping like crazy all the way. Ty opened the door looking serious.

Ty: Um, Alice is here.

Me: What?

Ty: Yeah, she just came over to pick something up... she didn't tell me in advance.

Alice appeared at the top of the steps.

Alice: Hi.

The temperature dropped like ten degrees from the way she looked at me.

Me: Hi. [whispering to Ty] We need to go.

Ty: [whispering back] I know.

Alice: What's going on?

Ty: Um, it's just – we need to go.

Alice: Right now? [she looked half-indignant, half-hurt.]

Ty: Yeah, we have to do... this thing...

Alice: [pinching her lips] You have to do a *thing*.

Ty looked at me nervously.

Me: You should tell her.

Ty nodded at me and took a deep breath. Before Alice could start speaking again, he filled her in as quickly as he could, and she listened with wide eyes. As soon as he was done, we started getting ready to go again.

Alice: I'm coming too.

Me: What?! No, what if it's dangerous, and there's already two of us—

Alice: —I'm coming too.

Ty: [sighing defeatedly] Ok, fine. Let's go.

As we walked over to the location of the pin on Google Maps, Ty filled in the story with more detail for Alice. He was having a hard time treading the line between giving me credit and also making it sound like we hadn't spent that much time together. He soldiered valiantly on every time she raised her eyebrows and said, 'I see...' in a pinched voice.

As we got close, we fell silent. The street we wanted was a cul-de-sac, and when we turned onto it there was no one around. It didn't look anything special. The houses weren't that nice and most of the little front gardens weren't tended to, but otherwise everything was perfectly normal. We strolled slowly past where the pin was positioned on the map. One of the houses had two broken windows and a *For Sale* sign.

Ty gestured towards a little space between two houses on the other side, and we followed him in. 'It's obviously the house that's for sale, right?'

'Yes,' I agreed.

From our hiding place, we could see the house clearly.

'It looks empty,' Ty said. 'Shall we just try going in?'

'No way,' Alice said.

'I thought we were just coming to check it out,' I said pointedly, but I already knew it wasn't going to turn out that way.

We watched the house. Nothing happened for ten minutes. We were completely silent. Alice didn't look at either of us, just mostly at her feet. The space was pretty squeezed, so my hand kept accidentally brushing hers. I nearly gave myself a cramp trying not to touch her. Ty wasn't looking at me either, so there we were, all three of us trying to avoid each other while standing in the tiniest space you could fit three people into. Very fun activity.

Finally, Ty whispered, 'I think we should do it, there's no one inside.'

'We don't know that for sure,' Alice said. 'Let's wait longer.'

The awkward silence resumed. I tried doing the Fibonacci sequence in my head to take my mind off the situation. Oh yes, I finally remembered to look it up just before I went to Ty's. The Fibonacci sequence starts with adding 1 and 1, and then you keep going by each time adding your new result to the one from just before:

$$1 + 1 = 2$$
$$1 + 2 = 3$$
$$2 + 3 = 5$$
$$3 + 5 = 8$$
$$5 + 8 = 13$$
$$8 + 13 = 21$$
$$...$$

It's often represented with the spiral shape that SPAM use. What you do is that you start with two 1-sided squares, side-by-side, and then each time you draw a new square whose side is the length of the two previous squares combined – adding the two previous numbers each time, just like in the sequence. You go around and around in a spiral, drawing a new square each time.

It starts off like this (where the numbers are showing the length of the side of each square):

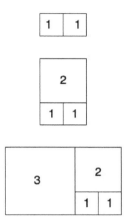

Then after a few more steps it looks like this:

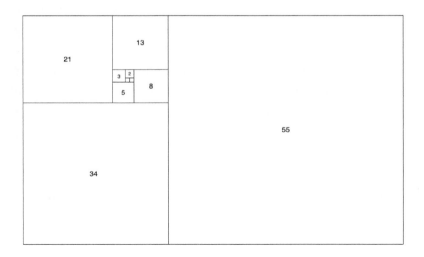

And then you draw the spiral, starting at the centre:

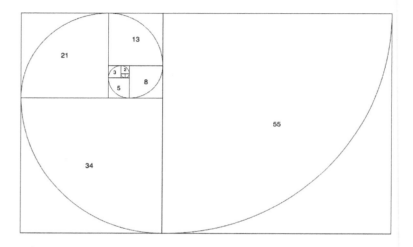

Doing the sequence in my head was actually a pretty effective way to pass the time. Several minutes passed less awkwardly than before and as I was doing 121393 + 196418, a man suddenly turned into the street. He walked down and stopped right in front of the house for sale, clearly waiting for something. We peered at him. Just like everything else around us, he looked exceedingly normal: medium height, brownish hair, wearing jeans. No hint of evil that I could see.

A couple of minutes later, two men came out of the house.

'See?' Alice said testily to Ty, who ignored her.

The men were wearing caps and scarves in such a way that we couldn't see their faces at all. One was a bit shorter than the other, but I couldn't have described them in any way. Either of them could have fit that grainy photo of Spencer that I had seen online.

We couldn't hear what they were saying, but after a little bit they all shook hands, and the two be-scarved men left. The remaining guy started pacing nonchalantly. It looked like he was discreetly keeping an eye on the house.

'Well, *now* we can go in,' Ty said.

'Yeah, I guess there's no one from SPAM left inside, since they have this guy here to keep a watch,' I agreed.

'He's obviously not a part of their group since he's not hiding his face,' Alice added. 'They must have just hired him.'

'So now… we just need to get past him.'

We all watched the man as he walked up to the top of the street and then back down again. He found a little wall to sit on and got his phone out. He seemed to have no inclination to move, and he was now pretty close to us. We waited in silence again, for how long I have no idea, but enough time to feel like this had been the worst idea in the history of ideas.

After a while, the man hopped off his little wall, put his phone in his pocket and stretched. He walked over to the house and into the front garden, glanced around to make sure no one was looking, unzipped his trousers and started peeing.

'Ew,' Alice said.

When he was done, he obviously felt the need to stretch his legs a bit, which I very much empathised with. He walked slowly up to the top of the street.

'I'm going to distract him,' Alice said decisively, stepping out.

'*Alice, wait! What are you doing?*' Ty whispered after her, but she was already sauntering up the street.

Alice was not at all wearing sweatpants. She had on some stretchy red trousers and a cropped pink shearling jacket. Her hair gleamed with the sheen of £300 salon visits. The guy, who had turned around immediately when he'd heard a sound, relaxed into a smile. Alice smiled back.

'Hello there,' the guy said to her.

'Hi,' Alice answered, charmingly.

'Do you live around here?'

'Yes, that house just there,' Alice said, pointing vaguely. 'Are you looking for something?'

She kept up a nonsense conversation, expertly manoeuvring around superficial subjects, making it sound like she was having the time of her life. Guess her dad had taught her a trick or two, unless smooth-talking is just a genetic trait.

Ty and I watched them until Alice had successfully got the guy to turn his back to us completely, at which point we dashed across the street and straight to the house. The front door was locked so I followed Ty round to the side of the house. He picked a stone off the ground.

'What's one more broken window,' he said, smashing the stone hard into the glass.

We heard the lookout guy's faint voice. 'Did you hear that?'

'Hear what?' Alice answered sweetly.

We waited silently for a few seconds but nothing happened, apart from my heart nearly exploding. Ty was buzzing, completely energised by this chance to pretend he was in an action movie, but meanwhile I felt more in danger of liquefying from fear. He reached a hand inside the hole he'd made, opened the window easily, lifted me inside and then followed.

The house was pretty grimy; there were only a few broken bits of furniture and a pile of unopened letters and flyers papering the entrance. Ty picked one up and showed me the postcode on it. We were in the right place. We didn't lose any time exploring – we were looking only for one thing, after all.

'Oli!' Ty shouted. 'Oli, are you here?'

'*Downstairs!*' we heard a tiny little voice.

Ty grabbed my arm, electrified.

We quickly found the door to the steps leading to the cellar and sprinted down them. We reached a little room with a couple of mattresses on the floor, plastic chairs, and a plastic table on which were strewn papers and two mugs with cold teabags in them. There was a door at the back of the room.

'*Ty! I'm in here!*' Oli said from behind the door.

'Oli!' Ty shouted with relief. He put his hand flat on the door. 'You're locked in? What happened?'

'Long story,' Oli said. 'The bigger question is what are *you* doing here?! You were supposed to send the police!'

'That's what I said!' I said.

'Who's that?' Oli asked.

'That's Clara,' Ty said quietly. 'She's my friend.'

'She's your *friend*, is she now?'

'Shut up,' Ty said. 'Let's work on getting you out of here. Then you can talk again, but it better be just to tell me everything that's happened!'

There was a keypad by the door, that would obviously unlock it.

'I haven't managed to see what the code is,' Oli said from behind the door. 'I just know that it's five digits, because I counted the number of the beeps. So it's not a date – that would be six digits, or eight if you write the year in full. And I imagine the keypad has been programmed so it shuts down if you get it wrong, 'cause that's what I would have done.' I could hear his grin and shrug in the way he talked.

'Ok,' I said. 'Let's look around for a clue.'

'Also,' Oli said, 'they have cameras all over, linked to their phones, so they're definitely on their way over by now.'

'Oh my god, you're not helping,' Ty said. He was frenetically pacing around.

'It's better to know the facts,' Oli said. 'You probably have ten minutes. Well, eight now. Listen Ty, you need to promise me – whatever happens, in eight minutes you guys are out of here.'

Ty stayed silent, obviously not planning to promise anything.

'Ty?' Oli prompted, but Ty still said nothing. 'Clara?' Oli said.

'We promise!' I said. Ty shot me a dark look, but I just shot him one back.

'Great,' Oli said. 'I'm going to consider this a binding agreement.'

Ty kept pacing. I looked at the papers that had been left on the desk. It looked like some draft anonymous letters, and some mathematical workings full of symbols that I didn't know. In the margins, someone had doodled the Fibonacci spiral again and again. I wondered... I mean, it would make sense, wouldn't it?

'Fibonacci!' I shouted, my articulacy seemingly vanished.

'Oooh,' Oli said from inside. 'Of course, the simplest answer is usually the right one. Spencer is *obsessed* with the idea of perfection, that's why he uses the Fibonacci spiral as his logo. In a way, the Fibonacci sequence represents a reach towards perfection. If F_n is the nth Fibonacci number, and F_{n+1} is the following Fibonacci number, then as n gets bigger and bigger, the ratio F_{n+1}/F_n gets closer and closer to the golden ratio.'

'The golden ratio?' Ty said, surprised. 'Like, the number that's found in lots of Leonardo da Vinci's paintings? The divine proportion?'

'Yes, that one,' Oli said. 'Alright, so there are five 5-digit Fibonacci numbers.'

I raised my eyebrows at Ty, who made a *yeah, I know* face, and then I wrote down as Oli dictated: 10946, 17711, 28657, 46368, 75025. I frowned at the piece of paper. 'I think five is too many to just try them all,' I said.

'Yeah,' Oli agreed. 'I don't know how many wrong tries you're allowed. Maybe not even one – as mentioned, Spencer isn't big on mistakes.'

'How do we know which is the right one?' Ty said.

'Well...' Oli said slowly. 'The most special Fibonacci numbers are the ones that are prime. For some reason, there are a lot of prime numbers that are also Fibonacci numbers, and no one is quite sure why. No one's managed to prove much about it, not even if there are an infinite number of Fibonacci primes. But anyway, that would be my bet. If one of the 5-digit Fibonacci numbers is a prime, which I don't actually know.'

'Ok,' I said. 'Well, that leaves out 10946 and 46368 which are even, and 75025 is divisible by 5.' I crossed them out.

'We're left with 17711 and 28657,' Ty said.

'Neither of them are divisible by any of the small primes,' Oli said, 'not the primes up to 11 in any case.'

'So let's start with 13, and then keep trying all the primes,' I said. I started writing down the list of prime numbers from 13 for Ty: 13, 17, 19, 23, 29, 31, 37, 41, 43, 47, 53, 59... I got stuck, and Oli helped me go on: 61, 67, 71, 73, 79, 83, 89, 97, 101, 103, 107, 109, 113, 127, 131, 137, 139, 149, 151, 157, 163, 167—

'That's as far as you need to go,' Oli said. 'The next prime is 173, and 173^2 is 29929, which is bigger than both of our numbers.'

'Ty, you take 17711, and I'll do the other one,' I said. You just divide it by all of these numbers in order, so 17711/13, then 17711/17, then 17711/19 and you keep going until you get a whole number as a result.'

We both got our phones out and found the calculators. A couple of minutes ticked by. I was sweating nervously, all the way to my fingertips, which was a hugely unhelpful for typing. The eight-minute mark was getting closer. Then, suddenly...

Ty: I have a whole number! 17711 is 89x199!

Me: I haven't found a whole number yet.

Oli: Well, if there is a prime Fibonacci with five digits, then it's yours, Clara. 28657.

Me: I could keep dividing to make sure. I've got to 101.

Ty: We don't have the time. And we don't have any other ideas anyway.

He typed the number in. I held my breath. The door made a soft click. We all froze.

'Oh my god,' Ty said under his breath. 'We did it.'

The door opened slowly to reveal Oli, who looked pretty much exactly like the photo I'd seen of him, if that photo was method-acting Robinson Crusoe: scraggly beard, dirty clothes and all.

Ty threw his arms around his brother's shoulders for a hug and Oli squeezed him back. When they broke apart, Ty's eyes were shiny and Oli's were twinkling. Oli looked me up and down.

'Hello there, Clara the *friend*,' he said and winked.

Ty rolled his eyes.

'Sadly, there is no time for this conversation right now,' Oli said. 'Let's get you guys out of here before Spencer comes back.'

'We're the ones getting *you* out of here,' Ty grumbled.

Oli was looking through the papers on the table.

'What are you doing?' Ty asked.

'Nothing,' Oli said. 'Hey, take some photos of this for me quickly. They took my phone away.' Ty took a few pictures of the papers, and then we all scrambled up the stairs.

'If we go out the back, I think we can go through the neighbour's garden and onto the parallel street,' I suggested.

We could hear Alice and the lookout guy talking, now right outside the front door. 'Come on, be honest,' Alice was saying. '*Handmaid's Tale* and *Love Island* are on at the same time – what do you pick?'

'Wait,' Oli looked confused. 'Is that... Alice?'

'Later,' Ty mumbled. 'I'll tell you later.'

We rushed out of the back door. There was a low gate to the adjoining house at the back which we climbed over and then ran across their garden and out into another small street, also a dead-end, that looked exactly like the one we'd just come from.

Suddenly, at the top of our street where it crossed the bigger one, the two guys from earlier ran past, in their scarves and caps. We ducked behind a bush until they disappeared. Oli and Ty looked at each other.

'You guys just go,' I said. 'I'll get Alice.' Oli looked at me, frowning. 'We'll be fine,' I insisted before he could say anything. No way we had done all of this for him to act all protective and get himself caught again.

Oli still didn't look happy, but there wasn't any time to argue. The two of them took off running, and I ducked back into the garden of a house lower down the street. My plan was to cut back to our cul-de-sac, towards the bottom. The SPAM guys still needed to get all the way down to the level of the *For Sale* house, and that gave me a few seconds' head start. I scrambled across, and when I stepped out, I could see that they had already turned the corner at the top of the street and were running down. There was no time to do any thinking.

'Alice!' I screamed.

She clocked me, a couple of houses down, and the SPAM guys running towards her from the other side, and took off in my direction. Wow, she was fast in heels.

We tore back across and into random streets, until I had to stop and fall to the ground wheezing. Alice is head of our handball team and she was barely sweating.

'Sorry,' I panted.

She crouched down next to me. 'I don't think they even tried to follow us,' she said.

'Yeah, I guess we're no use to them,' I said.

There was no sound at all around apart from rustling leaves and a few cars. Certainly no one running.

'We got Oli out,' I told her.

'Oh!' She clapped her hands together. She looked pleased.

'He and Ty ran off so they would be safe.'

My breathing was starting to go back to normal, but my heart was still really protesting this amount of exercise.

'Ok,' she said.

'You... You were amazing back there. With the guy.'

'I just wanted to help,' Alice said, her mouth set.

A silence settled in, one of those uncomfortable ones. She obviously had no plan to break it.

'Alice...' I said finally. 'I'm really sorry. For... you know. For everything.' I sure was having to apologise a lot lately.

'It's ok,' she said softly, looking at the ground. 'Ty and me... It wasn't great. I just hadn't totally accepted it yet.'

'But it wasn't a nice way for things to happen.'

'Yeah. No.'

'So I'm sorry. I mean it.' I looked at her, and she looked back.

'Ok,' she said.

Just then my phone made a sound, a very startling reminder of normal life. 'It's my dad,' I said. 'I'm meeting him for lunch at his restaurant. You know, you've been there...' I suddenly had an intense desire for her to like me. 'Do you want to come?' I suggested.

'I said it's ok,' Alice answered, 'not that I want to be your friend.' She was smiling though, a little. I smiled back.

'Got it,' I said, sitting up. 'I think I can decisively say that my heart isn't going to burst now. Shall we go?'

We walked together to the bus stop and waved goodbye. 'See you later,' I said.

'Yeah. See you in school.'

School – what a crazy thought. School seemed so far away. But suddenly I wasn't dreading it so much anymore, now that Alice and I were... well, I don't know *what* we were. Not friends, she'd made that clear, but partners-in-crime, at least. Or partners-against-crime.

I joined Dad just a little late, having had no time to change. 'Nice of you to make an effort,' he joked when I appeared.

'Just preparation for what we're about to do,' I countered, showing off my elasticated waistband.

'Fair play,' he admitted. 'Shall we get started?'

Dad disappeared off to the kitchen to let them know what we wanted to try – it was our official unveiling-a-new-menu ritual. I checked my phone quickly, but there was nothing at all from Ty. *What's going on??* I texted. I put my phone on vibrate and slipped it in my pocket where I would feel it if he wrote back.

Dad reappeared, carrying two plates. He put them down with a flourish. He'd made tasting plates of all the new stuff: soft-boiled quails' eggs with celery salt, whole artichoke with anchovy dressing to dip, an updated spaghetti al'amatriciana.

'Spaghetti al'amatriciana, really,' I said pointedly.

Dad looked embarrassed. 'Look,' he said. 'I'm... sorry.'

Great – having to apologise clearly runs in the family.

'I'm just no good talking about... that stuff.'

Wow, he was doing an awesome job at it too. M certainly wouldn't be any less concerned after I told her about this. I stared at him.

'Old relationships are confusing,' he said finally. 'Actually, your mother told me that you and Sam broke up. I'm sorry. He was a nice boy.'

Touché. I wasn't ready to talk to him about Sam at all. I guess that made us even – well played Dad. 'Wow, you and mum sure talk a lot,' I said.

'We do share a daughter.'

'Oh, so I guess the whole debacle was my fault!'

He laughed and took a bite of the pasta. 'It's time for spaghetti to just be spaghetti,' he said meaningfully.

It was like in a movie when the screenwriters have written something they think is really profound but you're not sure you get it. Dad seemed pleased with himself though.

I took a bite as well. 'Well, it's good,' I said, letting us both of the hook for this conversation.

He disappeared down the stairs to the kitchen again and I immediately got my phone out. It had been doing a lot of vibrating, but none of it was a message from Ty. I sent him a few more question marks.

Dad came back with new plates. He sat down and I felt my phone again. I tried to look at it discreetly under the table.

'No phones with food,' Dad said. A sacred rule of his.

'I know,' I said. 'Sorry'.

I put the phone back in my pocket. The message wasn't from Ty anyway. The phone immediately buzzed again.

'Clara!' Dad said. 'Your phone is non-stop!'

'I know, believe me,' I agreed. I swear, I don't think I've ever received so many messages in such a short amount of time.

'Make it be silent,' Dad said.

'It *is* silent,' I protested.

'No it's not, I can hear it every ten seconds: *bzzz, bzzz,*' Dad countered.

I had to do as he said (the last buzz hadn't been Ty either). I felt that I would die of stress from not knowing if Ty was writing to me but actually Dad ended up being quite fun and distracting, telling me about restaurant-staff drama and the next menu changes.

As soon as lunch was over, I checked my phone obsessively, but still nothing from Ty! Now I'm back home, on tenterhooks and going CRAZY.

Sunday 23rd October

Couldn't update last night because – well, you'll see!

Around 4pm yesterday I couldn't take being on my own anymore and I went over to M's. I was too edgy to leave my phone for even one second or be in a place where I might not hear it ringing, so we stayed in her room. I'd already told her what had happened of course, but she made me go through it all again. She was extremely unimpressed about the fact that Alice had been with us. 'Alice? *Alice?*' She kept saying, as if somehow repeating the name would make it go away.

Even after I'd finished telling her the whole story again in minute detail, Ty still hadn't texted. M was becoming as crazy as me, asking every two seconds if I'd had a new message. I was getting a bit scared, wondering if SPAM had somehow managed to get to Ty and Oli after we'd separated. M managed to talk me down and to distract ourselves we picked through a pile of old magazines that Amanda had brought back from the waiting room of her hospital. They were many years old.

I sat on the floor with my back against the bedframe reading an old *Cosmopolitan* magazine with one eye, while I checked my phone with the other. It had a picture of Scarlett Johansson on the cover, photoshopped until she looked like Amber Heard. She was wearing an inconsistent outfit of a hooded wool jacket and high-waisted glittery hotpants; across her left hip you could read: *103 new ways to pleasure him* and just below, in a different font, *Why you don't need sex.*

M lay on her back on the bed, holding a ripped *Grazia* over her head. She kept giggling. Finally, she flipped the last page over, sighed and rolled onto her stomach. 'Any new messages?' I shook my head no. 'Well, at least this was very informative,' she said, shaking the magazine. 'Apparently the Kardashians invented cornrows. What about you – learn anything good?' She grabbed my phone to take a photo of the article for her Instagram.

'I'm learning all about what goes on in boys' heads,' I told her. 'This article is titled *The real reason we broke up.* Guys explain what they told their girlfriends when breaking up with them, but then they reveal the secret real reason.'

'Oh wonderful. Hit me.'

'So, this guy says: *I told her I wasn't looking for a serious relationship but actually I was angry because she had just died her hair dark brown. She had beautiful blonde hair that she knew I loved but she did it anyway. I didn't fancy her anymore after that.*' I looked at her. 'He was a real catch, that one.'

'My goodness, he's clearly crazy,' M deadpanned. 'Brunettes are obviously way better.'

I laughed and handed her the *Cosmo* so she could take a photo of my article too. There was a knock on the door, and Amanda poked her head in.

'What are you girls laughing at?' she asked.

'Oh, we're just reading through the old magazines you gave me before I throw them out,' M told her.

Amanda kneeled next to me and started flipping through a 2012 edition. 'Wow,' she said to herself. 'It's crazy how quickly these have become dated, isn't it?' She turned the page she was looking at round so we could look at it: *What to wear on a first date: guys reveal what your outfit makes them think of you.*

'Oh my god,' M scoffed and took another photo.

Amanda looked at the magazine again. 'You know, when I was your age, this type of magazine was a life-saver. We didn't have the internet, and we couldn't talk to our parents. Or I certainly couldn't, in any case.'

'Weren't you angry that it was all about how to look pretty and get a guy though?'

'Well, we were already having interesting conversations amongst ourselves. We didn't need magazines to teach us that.

Besides, we *did* want to look pretty and get guys. And I can't tell you how exciting it was to see the words *penis* or *clitoris* in print.'

'*Mum,*' M said.

'What? You should be pleased that I say these words freely. Your grandma never did.'

'Yes, we know, you're a *cool mom,*' M rolled her eyes.

'Oh, that's from that movie, isn't it? I know you're making fun of me,' Amanda laughed. 'I'm just saying – I think it's amazing that you girls can see how ridiculous these magazines are and it's amazing that new magazines are being created that don't talk to women in the same way, and that appreciate the whole range of experiences that women have, and the sexuality spectrum too. But these old magazines served a real feminist purpose at one point in time. You shouldn't forget that.' She raised both her hands. 'Your generation, you just throw everything out. Seminal feminist writers, who inspired hundreds of thousands of women: they say one thing you don't like and they're in the bin.'

'It's not just saying one thing we don't *like,*' M scowled.

'I don't agree with her any more than you do, but how you can simply forget about everything she's done is... oh!' Amanda interrupted her own thought, on a roll now. She gets exactly the same look in her eyes that M does when she's fired up about something. 'You throw out everything you don't like, but then there are some things that inexplicably get rehabilitated! Clara, maybe you can explain this to me – Miracle is crazy for this book that my girlfriends and I all hated when it came out – the Chris Kraus one that's been re-edited to look all trendy, you know: *I Love Dick*. I mean, apart from the obvious appeal in reading a book with that title on the tube, what is it that you girls like about it?'

'Um,' I said. 'I guess it feels really revolutionary to allow a female character to be... not perfect.'

'To be smart and difficult and incisive and infuriating. To be simultaneously involved and complicit in her own unfeminist existence, but also rage against it,' M added. Yeah, she's better at this than me. 'Perfect feminist heroes are great, but most of us have grown up in this sexist world and we can't help but have internalised some of it – it's much more realistic, it represents us.'

'But she's a stalker. And a mess. When the book came out, my friends and I, we were just like... get it together, woman!' Amanda said. 'We certainly didn't feel that she represented us.'

'Men are celebrated for being messes all the time. Like in *The Hangover*, or all the old-timey book with their "loveable rogues".' M made air quotes with her fingers. 'It's about time women are too. And really, Mum… we *are* messes. I've done stupid things. Stupid, unfeminist things.' She glanced at me.

'So have I,' I said quietly.

'Whatever you girls do, you are wonderful, smart treasures,' Amanda said and scooped us up for a hug.

'That's the point, Mum,' M said from inside Amanda's arms. 'Both those things are true at the same time. I mean, *you*'ve definitely been a mess, whatever you say.'

Amanda laughed. 'But it created you! It wasn't a mess, it was destiny.'

'You tell yourself that,' M rolled her eyes.

'Well, you're certainly good at arguing,' Amanda said. 'But for me, a book that makes me despise its central female character can't call itself feminist.'

'It doesn't *call itself* feminist,' M protested.

'My mum would agree with you Amanda,' I shrugged. 'She's like, "I'm a scientist without a home-making bone in my body, and your dad cooked every meal that was eaten in our house and looked after you more than I did. If you want to be a feminist, stop complaining about the patriarchy and just live a feminist life." That's a verbatim quote from when I wanted her to come to the women's march.'

Amanda laughed, but M was having none of it. 'Whatever,' she said. 'You guys were progressive for your time, but the world is different now. There was a time when saying women should be allowed to wear *trousers* was revolutionary. In fifty years, you'll just be the old ladies still proud of wearing trousers back when it was illegal. Meanwhile, we'll have shepherded in a new feminism – radical, inclusive, intersectional, concerned with more than just itself.'

'What she said!' I said. Amanda gave a little mock applause.

Music streamed through the door she'd left open. The up-stairs neighbours were making an incomprehensible racket, seemingly jumping up and down in irregular patterns whilst all wearing clogs. It was like being back in the summer for a moment, when I spent all of my free time with M, I barely knew Ty, Sam and I were planning to have sex and I didn't know Oli existed – I think I actually genuinely forgot to think about my phone for a moment. In any case, when it rang, I nearly jumped out of my skin.

M was still holding it, and she glanced at the screen. 'It's Ty!' she screamed. 'Mum, go away!'

'Why, who is this Ty?' Amanda asked.

'Just go away!' M shouted and pushed her towards the door. Amanda left, giggling wildly to herself, and I picked up.

'Hi,' I said breathlessly.

'Hi,' Ty said back.

'Oh my god!' I exclaimed, 'I've been going crazy! What happened to you guys?'

'I'm sorry. They took my phone. GCHQ, I mean.'

I breathed out for what felt like the first time all day. 'I'm so glad you're ok. I had a lot of terrifying scenarios going round my head!'

'I'm really sorry,' Ty said again. 'I didn't have a single chance to text. When we got home, we told our parents what had happened, and they called the GCHQ guys who came right away and took my phone away to check if it had been hacked. Then they made us take them to the house Oli was kept in and everything. We've only just got back.'

'Ok,' I said. 'Well, now you have to tell me everything, every little detail!'

'What's happening?' M demanded to know.

'They're back home,' I told her, and she did a little clap.

'Are you with M?' Ty's voice asked in my ear.

'Yes,' I told him, 'I'm at her house.'

'You should come over now,' Ty said.

'Really, won't your parents mind that I'm crashing if I come?'

'No, of course not,' he said, 'they want you here. I told them how much you helped.'

'Can I come?' M mouthed at me, making wild gestures with her arms. 'I want to come!'

'Umm... can I bring M?' I asked in the phone.

'I also helped!' M shouted so that Ty would hear. 'With the Kanter thing!'

'It's true,' I said, 'I would never have got that irrational infinity question without her.'

Ty laughed. 'Yes, she can come.'

I made a thumbs-up at M, and I swear I heard her mutter under her breath, '*Take that, Alice.*'

When I hung up, I squealed and excitedly hugged M. We rushed out at triple speed.

'I'll explain later, Mum!' M shouted to Amanda as we closed the door behind us and ran all the way to the bus stop.

The scene at Ty's was a joyful mess, with everyone talking at the same time. I'd felt really shy coming in, meeting Ty's parents for the first time, but they were so happy and welcoming that I forgot to be nervous right away. There was a mountain of pizza boxes on the table, enough for a group double the size of ours.

'Thank you so much for coming, girls!' Ty's mum exclaimed. 'You'll have to help us with all of this.' She gestured at the heaving table.

'We'll help, but I want to hear the whole story first,' I said. 'You need to tell me everything that happened after you guys ran off!'

I was still feeling a bit trembly from those hours with no news, though having Ty in my line of sight helped (being able to touch him constantly would have been better, but... parents).

'Well,' Ty said. 'As soon as we got home and told Mum and Dad what had happened, they called GCHQ, hoping there would still be a chance to catch the SPAM guys. We took them to the house, but of course there was nothing at all left there by time we arrived – they'd cleaned the whole house out.'

'I can't believe these people tricked Oli into going over there so they could lock him up. Pure evil,' Ty's mum shuddered.

Ty shot me and M an urgent look. Evidently, some details were being kept from the parents. I nodded as a promise that we'd stick to the story.

'Only, at the same time as Oli worked on the bank hack, he was also figuring out how to send us the code,' Ty continued. 'He said that it took him almost a week to get through the bank's security, and then a few more days to figure out how he could put money into some bank accounts to send us a message. Hey, where is Oli?' Ty frowned. He looked around for his brother, who had mysteriously vanished.

'I'm here,' Oli said, re-entering.

He'd been in the bathroom, and his previously wild beard was now a rugged stubble. He'd changed into a worn denim shirt with a patched-up tear on the wrist. His eyes seemed to always be laughing, whereas Ty's were usually serious, but otherwise they looked a lot like each other.

'Were we meant to see your message when the news broke?' I asked.

'Actually,' Oli said, 'the people I sent the code to were all people we know. Mum's brother, Dad's editor, a friend of mine

- all the people I could find who had accounts with that bank. I hoped that one of them would notice and tell you about it, and you would put the two together. Or rather, mum and dad would put the two together after you'd told them everything.' He said that last part under his breath, so that only Ty and I could hear.

'Well then don't leave a note saying to please not tell them', Ty said out of the corner of his mouth. Out loud, he said 'hey, you cleaned up! I thought you were enjoying your kidnap-victim look!'

'Yeah, well...' Oli looked away. Was he... blushing a bit? He came towards me. 'Nice to meet you more properly, Clara. So you're the one who solved my maths problems? Unfortunately, it seems that even me going through this whole ordeal wasn't enough to awaken Ty's mathematical gene.'

'It was me. Sorry,' I said.

'Don't be sorry, you did *save* me. I suppose I'd pick that over Ty understanding countable infinity – only just.'

'Oli, shut up,' Ty protested, but he squeezed my shoulder happily.

Turns out that happy Ty is even hotter than worried Ty, by the way. I was seriously regretting not getting changed before rushing over. My outfit of old Levi's and one of dad's T-shirts was perfect for lounging on M's bed but not so much for the current situation. I really should have been reading those *Cosmo* articles more carefully – surely there must have been a section on the perfect outfit to wear when the brother of the guy you're seeing has just returned from being locked up by a hacker gang. I tried to surreptitiously tuck the T-shirt inside the waistband of my jeans so that at least I would regain a waist.

'What? I've only just escaped dangerous kidnappers and you already want me to shut up?' Oli exclaimed. Then he turned to M, and suddenly the reason for the shave and outfit change became clear. 'And you're...?'

I watched as M shook herself into action, sashayed towards him with a flick of her hair and her right arm extended. 'I'm Miracle,' she said.

Oli blinked in agreement, looking as if he had just found the solution for one of those million-dollar maths problems. I rolled my eyes forcefully at M but she shrugged me off and discreetly undid the top button of her shirt.

We sat down around the table and started opening the pizza boxes, handing around slices. Oli inhaled his like someone who's been locked in a basement for days.

'Can I have some of that one over there,' he gestured vaguely towards Ty. 'The ham and cheese one.'

'They're all ham and cheese,' Ty said.

'That one! The red ham with the white soft cheese.'

'Prosciutto and ricotta,' Ty and I said in unison, which made Oli laugh.

'In Clara's defence,' M said, 'her dad is a chef.'

'I see,' Oli said. 'Ty has no such excuse, he's just someone who reads cookbooks like they are actual books.'

'At least I read actual books,' Ty shot back.

'I read books,' Oli looked affronted.

'...that don't have spaceships in them,' Ty said.

'What a snob,' Oli said. 'Food and books... What's next, are you going to start critiquing my outfits?'

'Well actually...' Ty said, and everyone laughed.

It was amazing how different the flat felt from the times I'd been before. It had transformed into a completely happy place. Ty and Oli couldn't stop smiling. Both parents kept looking at Oli with the wonder and amazement normally bestowed on a newborn baby. Ty's dad twinkled as he tried to get more of the story out of Oli, who was too busy showing off to answer his questions. Ty's mum was positively radiant – she moved around like she was floating.

Actually, Ty has that exact same way of moving – like a really elegant puppet. I can't really describe it. It's like all the bits of their bodies are joined up in a much more loose and continuous way than normal people. I'd noticed it before, when Ty would lift his mattress to reach for the laptop under it. Normally people look awkward lifting up a mattress, but when he did it everything just clicked into place and it looked like the most natural thing to do. It made my insides tight watching him get up to grab a clean glass from the cupboard or pick the now-empty pizza boxes off the table. I couldn't stop thinking about him touching me in that same smooth way.

Since we'd had sex, which felt like *forever* ago, I'd constantly been just half a level below extremely horny, which was very distracting when attempting to go about the day. Any time my brain wasn't 100% fully engaged on something, it would immediately turn to things like Ty's tongue circling my nipple, or his fingers trailing up my thighs, and I'd miss my bus stop or find that I'd been staring through the window for twenty minutes. Our eyes caught and Ty smiled, liquefying me further.

I shook my head and turned back to Oli. I had so many questions still! 'What did the GCHQ guys say when you suddenly appeared?'

'Oh, they were relieved,' Oli said lightly. 'GCHQ know all about SPAM obviously – they've been after Spencer for years.'

'So they knew SPAM were involved the whole time?' I asked. 'We thought they were after you!'

'I wish they'd told us,' Ty's mum said. 'It was a horrible shock seeing them on our doorstep, like we'd gone back five years in the past.'

'I'm sorry, Mum.' Oli put his hand on his mother's arm.

Out of the corner of my eye I noticed Ty shoot me a look. He was looking at Oli strangely, and then at me, as if trying to send me a message, but I didn't know what.

M hadn't noticed the looks. 'What was it like being in that basement for days?' she asked, leaning way over the table.

Oli seemed glad for the change of topic. 'It wasn't much fun, I'll be honest. All of them wore masks all the time so I didn't see another human face for days. And the only time I even saw anyone was when they came in to give me food.'

This was the first I'd seen Oli be serious, and he looked exhausted all of a sudden, a shadow over his face. Then his parents started making worried noises, and he went back to his old self.

'The stuff they were feeding me was even worse than my own cooking!' he laughed.

'No!' his mum exclaimed.

'Yes, Mum. I can only assume there was a deal on the frozen diet-food section, because everything was *lean* this and *no-fat* that. I tell you, one of my legendary peanut butter and pickle sandwich would have been mighty good at that point.'

We all groaned with disgust. Well, except for M.

'Peanut butter and pickle is a classic!' she exclaimed.

Oli beamed at her.

'What did you *do* all day long?' I asked.

'I pretty much worked all day,' Oli explained. 'The bank was always fighting back against what I was doing, so I had to keep changing my method.'

'And SPAM picked you because you'd hacked that bank before?'

'Yes. They easily found out that I was behind the old hack, even if my name had never been published.' His mum scowled.

'Getting past the bank's security was way more difficult this time!' Oli exclaimed, looking almost excited. 'They had added lots of extra protection. I had to bypass at least twenty different levels of—' he stopped abruptly there, having noticed his dad's very unimpressed face. Instead, he told us that he'd been convinced into doing the bank job because Spencer threatened to hack into the A-level results and stop Ty from getting into university. The looks of horror on their parents' faces was quite a sight – M couldn't stop giggling.

'Can *you* hack into the A level results?' Ty asked. 'Or is it just Spencer who can?'

'Why, you need some help?'

'Well, you know, I *have* been quite distracted lately,' Ty said.

'This joking isn't funny,' their dad interrupted. 'Some jokes are funny but not this one.'

'Ah yes,' Oli turned to M and me. 'Our dad is the absolute world authority on what jokes are funny.'

We both laughed, in M's case twinkling extra hard. The boys' parents got up to take our empty plates to the kitchen and switch to dessert – ice cream from the pizza place. The conversation moved on – ranking the ice-cream flavours, movies that had come out in the two weeks Oli was gone…

Ty leaned towards me and cocked his head, eyebrows raised, towards M, who was listening with rapture to Oli saying stuff about software and cryptocurrency.

'*I know,*' I mouthed.

By the time we finished dinner and anyone looked at the time, it was nearly midnight. Ty's parents were starting to look tired and I suddenly felt bad that we'd been hanging around and not letting them have time alone with their son, whose attention, let's be honest, was focussed at least 72% on just one person.

'We really should go, I'm sorry it's so late,' I said, starting to make our excuses.

'It's been just wonderful having you girls over,' Ty's mum said.

'Absolutely wonderful,' Oli concurred. '*Miraculous*, even. A marked improvement on the company you kept previously, Ty. Does this mean I won't be subjected to conversations with Alice and her Miss India sidekick anymore?'

M giggled, and Ty punched his brother's arm. He looked at me awkwardly, which Oli laughed at. Oli seems to find awkwardness very enjoyable.

Their mum looked at Oli. 'I've asked you already not to talk like this about Rayna.'

Oli looked over at us. 'Mum is very protective of Rayna. She remains mysterious about the details, but it seems that Rayna's parents were mean to her once at temple.'

'There are no details. I just think Rayna needs good friends, that's all. Her parents are… not very nice people.'

'That's probably because you go to the events at the temple only like once every three years,' Oli teased, and his mum shushed him.

M and I exchanged looks. This was all very interesting of course, but even in my happy state I wasn't sure that I would be able to consider the words *Rayna* and *friend* in the same sentence. M silently agreed with me through the medium of her eyebrows.

'Well, thanks so much for everything. The pizza, and…' I gestured vaguely, trying to move the conversation in another direction.

'Wait – Clara can you stay?' Ty said, to my amazement. He turned round to his parents. 'Can she stay?'

'Oh yes, of course,' his mum said.

'Um,' Oli interjected. 'I was always told that only official girl-friends are allowed to stay over.'

'That's true,' their dad added with a twinkle. 'Only official girlfriends.'

'Yup. Clara's my girlfriend,' Ty said.

I willed my mouth to stay closed. M secretly poked me in the ribs.

Oli grinned. 'Welcome to the family then, Clara the *girl-friend*.'

'Well that's settled then,' their mum said, shooting Oli a warning look. He definitely earned a lot of those.

Ty's parents insisted on calling M an Uber before they went to their bedroom. While we were waiting for it, I hugged her goodbye. We had some more eyebrow discussion about the girl-friend comment.

'Um, so I'll be texting my mum to tell her I'm staying at yours,' I said in a low voice.

'Expected as much,' she agreed. 'Have fun! Come see me to-morrow and tell me everything.'

'I will,' I promised.

She waved goodbye to everyone and then she was off. Oli's parents insisted on walking him to his bedroom, to his evident annoyance. Ty stared at his brother's back as he left us in front of the door.

'They won't leave him on his own,' he laughed.

'They'll relax.'

'Yes, I guess so. In the meantime it's annoying, I still have lots of questions for him that I can't ask.'

'About what really happened?' I whispered. 'Why he went to meet SPAM?'

'Yes,' he whispered back. 'But also – did you see how he avoided answering your questions about GCHQ? There's something going on there, I know it!'

Oh, so that's what that look had been about. 'He'll tell you when the two of you are on your own,' I said. 'For now, why don't you enjoy not having any secrets for just a few hours?'

Ty laughed. 'Very good suggestion,' he agreed. He grabbed my hand and we went to his bedroom. As soon as we were inside, he said, 'By the way, I only said that earlier so my parents would let you sleep here. About being my girlfriend, I mean. We don't have to... you know.'

'It's fine,' I said. 'I quite enjoyed it.'

'You did?'

'Yes. I mean, we can keep it just for parents. For now.'

'Deal.' He laughed. 'You looked gorgeous at dinner,' he said. 'Very distracting.'

'What? In this sexy outfit?'

'Not the outfit. *You* looked gorgeous.'

He kissed me again. Wow. *Yes*, I thought. *Yes*, my whole entire body thought. The kissing was making my insides dance around. I tugged at his T-shirt to pull it off.

'Wow, ok,' he breathed with a smile.

'Yeah,' I whispered back.

We half-undressed each other. Every bit of my skin Ty touched felt hot hot hot.

'Hey,' he said in a kissing break, 'I wanted to ask you some-thing. Would you show me how you do it... when you're on your own? I want to learn what you like.'

'Ok,' I said, though I felt quite self-conscious. I started unbuttoning my trousers, and Ty helped me pull them off. Then he pulled my pants off too. I must have looked pretty much like how I felt, and I think he noticed.

'I'll get naked as well,' he said, and got undressed. He kissed me again softly and then more urgently and I closed my eyes. That was a lot better.

We lay down on the bed and I started moving my fingers on myself, as Ty kissed down my neck and to my breasts. Slowly, everything ebbed away from around us until there was only his lips and his hands and my fingers, and the most incredible sensation deep inside my stomach. I could feel myself getting really close, but then Ty shifted his position slightly and suddenly the thought crossed my mind that this had been going on for ages. Surely Ty was getting bored or wondering if there was something wrong with me. I landed squarely back on Earth, and the harder I tried to get back into it, the more I got worried about how long I was taking.

'Ty,' I whispered after a bit.

'Yes?'

'I'm just – I'm sorry, it feels incredible, but I think I'm a bit nervous and I can't...'

'Hey, that's fine,' he said. 'Maybe... do you want to me to show you instead?'

'Yes,' I said. 'I'd like that'.

Ty lay on his back and started masturbating. He alternately closed his eyes and stared at me. His breathing got quicker. 'Give me your hand,' he stuttered. I put my hand in his outstretched one and he placed it at the base of his penis and moaned.

That did it – I felt very, extremely horny again. His every muscle was tensed and there was a thin sheen of sweat on his torso and above his lip. He looked like a perfect gleaming statue. I shifted to be on my back again and started touching myself with my free hand (which was the right one, fortunately). Ty opened his eyes and smiled at me.

The rest was... The rest was... amazingly amazing. We came at the exact same time, I swear. I felt his body shudder all over, matching mine. It felt like... oh my god, this is so corny – I'm never showing this to M. It felt like we were just one body. One perfect, beautiful body. Really, I felt such a wonderful, warm feeling about everything, Ty's perfect eyelashes and my perfect hands and the way we fitted perfectly together. It was completely life-changing – until a minute passed and my hands felt clammy and I needed to pee and I noticed Ty was holding the T-shirt he'd grabbed to ejaculate into awkwardly over the side of the bed. And I worried about how my breasts looked when I was lying down. Back to normal, then.

When I came back from going to the loo and washing my face, Ty was already half-asleep. He pulled me to his hot, damp chest, kissed my shoulder and murmured something unintelligible, then released me and turned to face the other way. I proceeded to not sleep a wink because of the strangeness of being in a bed with someone else. (I mean, I sleep ok with M, in between her kicking me. But with her I don't get shaken awake every time sleep starts to descend by the fear that she will open her eyes to see me drooling on the pillow.)

I watched the light behind Ty's curtains get lighter slowly. I guess I did fall asleep at some point because I was woken up when he got out of bed and crept outside. I checked my phone. A couple of calls from Mum, and a text.

M: *Yo. How was your big night with Ty??!!!!!!!!(!!!) Your mum called but I told her you were still asleep. Tell me everything. Send me pics.*

I took a quick selfie and sent it to her (her phone gets photos as these extremely pixellated videogame-looking images, which she claims she is happy about).

Me: *Ty's bed.*

M: *!!!Sex hair!!! Come over – I want all the details!*

Me: *I'll go home to shower and change and then I'll come to yours.*

I looked at the photo again – she was right about the hair, wow. I brushed my hands through it quickly and rubbed traces of sleep out of my eyes. I hopped out of bed and pulled my clothes on before Ty came back in with a glass of water.

'Hey.' He smiled, offering me the glass. The water tasted extremely delicious. 'Do you want some breakfast?' Ty asked. 'We're on our own. Oli messaged to say that they've gone out for food, just the three of them. My parents are obviously not planning to let him out of their sight yet.'

I was pretty happy to hear that no one else was in as I wasn't feeling quite ready to face a room full of family members in my first morning-after moment. 'Actually, I think I should go home,' I said. 'My mum's been calling and I haven't exactly told her where I am...'

Ty laughed. 'Ok,' he said. 'Shall we... go to the cinema to-morrow? Or do I need to find more maths problems to lure you over?'

'Well, that depends on your taste in films,' I said.

'I guess I can always just do this.'

He kissed me softly and slid his hand from between my shoulder blades to my lower back and then the top of my bum.

He pulled me closer towards him and my legs started feeling like jelly.

'Oh my god!' I whisper-exclaimed.

He laughed and held his hands up. 'You can go.' He walked me to the door and gave me one last kiss.

'Tell me if you do manage to talk to Oli,' I said as I left.

I messaged Mum to tell her I was on my way home, and she sent me a photo of the kitchen table laid with pancakes, Emma smiling hungrily. *I'm running as fast as I can!* I sent back.

I made it back in time to join their second round. I discreetly enquired about John's whereabouts and was told that the cyber attack had been stopped but John's problems weren't over as the *Mail on Sunday* had just published a pretty damning piece, plus all efforts to recuperate money had so far been in vain. He was therefore back at the office.

The three of us didn't let any of this impact our brunching, however, and I'm writing this full of pancakes before I go see M, who has been enthusiastically preparing a range of activities for us now that uni applications and saving Oli are both done with and we have only the small matter of A Levels to take up our time.

Monday 24th October

Extremely hungover. I somehow had the presence of mind last night to come back to Dad's instead of Mum's. Very prescient of me because I was sick three times when I woke up and Dad just laughed and brought me coconut water and a cheese toastie and then left me alone again, whereas Mum would be… Oh, I don't know. Whatever she'd have done, it would have been torture. Though I have since dragged myself over to hers because the shower is better.

A DJ that M likes was playing at a club in Dalston last night. I tried to remind M that we'd only recently sat through a speech about the importance of studying in half-term, but she didn't even dignify this with a response. She also vetoed my daytime outfit as going to get us ID'd and I didn't feel like going home to change, so she made me wear her vintage silver nightie with pale-blue tights.

'No trainers,' she declared.

'But I can't wear any of your shoes,' I protested. M has size-8 feet like a penguin.

She waved me quiet. 'I'll get something of my mum's.'

Five minutes later she returned with platform shoes in the exact same blue as the tights. I put them on and instantly looked much better than I ever had before in my life.

'Wow, thanks,' I said. 'Wow,' I repeated.

'I know,' M shrugged.

She herself looked like a mermaid who'd sold her voice for a pair of legs in a transparent green dress and patent boots. She handed me a brown lipstick. Bouncers always think you're two years older than you are when you wear lipstick. Except if it's pink. M went for a bright red.

We took the bus, bundled into long coats that made us look demure. There was a group of guys sitting at the front of the top deck, talking loudly at each other across the aisle and sipping from forbidden cans. M asked them if we could have one and they could only acquiesce, stricken dumb by her appearance.

The bouncer at the door didn't even look twice at us when we walked in. I walked past him with my heart beating all the way into my toes but we could have been ghosts for the amount of attention he paid us.

It reminded me of the time M and I went to Sainsbury's, picked up a few things and walked straight out the door. We even told the security guy we hadn't paid for anything. He just nodded at us and smiled. 'See, you can do anything if you just act confidently,' M said, which is pretty much her life motto. We had a picnic with the stuff we'd stolen.

We started a bit of a life of crime after that, stealing jewellery from Claire's Accessories (just to be clear, we were eleven years old and this was considered the height of style). You know, it feels like stealing from Claire's is the safer thing to do, as opposed to, say, stealing from the Selfridges jewellery counter, but it's really not. They have proper security people in that place. They look at you suspiciously whatever you're doing. Then again, they can't be very good at what they do because whenever you go to pick up one of those packs of earrings, half of them are gone.

Anyway, M would do this thing where she'd behave quite suspiciously, looking at a million things at once, pulling stuff off the hooks and attracting attention. Plus, the security guys were always way more interested in her than in me anyway. 'Might as well use this racial profiling situation to our advantage,' she said. So, she'd act suspicious and then eventually put everything back where she'd found it and walk out. Meanwhile, I'd pick two things, one for her and one for me, and stuff them in my pocket. M waited for me at a pre-arranged location.

What she didn't know was that I always felt too bad about the stealing so I would go to the counter and pay for one of the pieces. The way I saw it, I was paying for mine, and the stolen one was M's. She never felt guilty, so it was fine to think of it that way. Anyway, I admitted it to her one time and she was beside herself laughing. She made me walk back to the store to take something without buying anything else. And just then, as we were going back in, two girls were walking out innocently, one of the security guys leaped after them and sure enough, their pockets were bursting full of sparkly stuff. There were a lot of tears, parents were called, everything.

'Amateurs,' M said. 'We'd never get caught.'

But neither of us ever felt like doing it again.

Sneaking into a club is better anyway. You get the same goosebump feeling and you win a party, instead of some bad jewellery (though I did love my dolphin mood ring).

The beer we'd shared on the bus felt nice and tingly on an empty stomach. Inside, M got us a double rum and ginger to share. The dancing was down a flight of stairs and it was hot and damp like a jungle in there. We abandoned our coats on a sofa in a corner and pushed through people to the middle of the dancefloor. I think it was all uni students apart from us, which would make sense given it was a Sunday. I can't believe we'll be them just next year.

For a couple of hours we just danced, got one more drink to share, and then were bought one each by a very awesome-looking girl who came over to say she liked our outfits. She told us she was a student at King's and M got excited that they might know each other next year.

Things got a little hazy. The music was really great. M was getting to her swaying, expansive stage. She leant over to me.

'I'm going to tell my mum,' she said, 'about Leo'.

'Oh M,' I said. I put my arms around her. 'I think that's good.'

'I just need a few more days, I think.'

'Well, I'll be here. Forever and ever.'

I squeezed her as tight as I could.

We danced more. My feet hurt a lot because Amanda's feet are a size bigger than mine and the thick socks M had given me weren't quite making up the difference. Also, the platforms were about three inches higher than my own highest heels.

The music was good enough that I managed to ignore the pain for a long time. After a while though I told M I had to take a break upstairs in the smoking area, and she said she'd come with me. We walked up the stairs, out the back and ran smack into Sam. Sam with his face glued to a girl. I gawped in shock.

'Sam!' M exclaimed, which caused the two of them to get unglued.

'Oh my god – Clara!' Sam said in turn. My vision was pretty blurry and he kept his face so still it was hard to tell if he was horrified or fine or pleased. 'Hi!'

'Hi,' I said.

'Hi,' the girl said. 'I'm Julie.' She was blonde and small and quick to blush.

'It's so crazy to run into to you here,' M said, when it became clear that neither Sam nor I had recovered the power of speech yet.

'Oh, yes. Julie's uncle...'

'My uncle manages the DJ,' Julie jumped in after Sam's voice had trailed off into an embarrassed mumble.

'No way!' M practically shouted. 'I love her! I'm obsessed with her! That is beyond cool!' I glared at her but she ignored me.

'Oh, well... I can get you guys some VIP wristbands if you like,' Julie shrugged, blushing again. 'We can go into the DJ booth.'

'Are you kidding!' M squealed like a banshee. 'That would be amazing! You're the best!!!' M squeezed my wrist, oblivious to my glowering. 'Oh my god I'm so excited!'

308 - CORALIE COLMEZ

'I didn't know who she was until tonight,' Julie said, positively scarlet now. 'But my uncle said she was good so...'

They disappeared inside to get the wristbands, leaving Sam and me on our own.

'So...' I said.

'So,' Sam said.

'So, um. Julie...'

'Um yeah. We're not, like, going out or anything. She invited me tonight and...'

'Hey, it's fine if you are going out with her,' I said.

'But I'm not,' he insisted.

He actually didn't seem that enthused about the prospect. That's not just me being snarky, I swear. He really didn't seem enthused. Which in turn made me feel more generous.

'Well. She seems great,' I said.

'Yeah.'

There was a silence. I willed M to reappear, but she didn't. It was horrible feeling so awkward with Sam. It was completely wrong. I was about to suggest going inside when Sam started talking again.

'Clara… I saw all your messages. I was just too angry to answer.' He looked down at the ground.

'I get it,' I said. 'I am so sorry. I'm so sorry about what I did. You would be right to never speak to me again.'

(More apologising. Dare I say that I hope this will be the last time I do something that necessitates apologies for a good while? I'm on quite a bad run these days.)

'That was sort of my plan,' he sighed. 'But now, bumping into you, I guess… It feels like it's nice to see you, you know?'

I nodded.

'I sort of wish I did feel angry at you but instead I just feel like I want to hang out again.'

'I really want to keep hanging out. I've been wanting to tell you so many things. You have no idea how crazy my family has been. My dad called you a nice boy, though.'

Sam smiled. 'That's great, maybe he can write me a reference for the next—' He stopped there and I was grateful. Turns out I wasn't quite ready for this yet. Sam was obviously feeling the same. 'Maybe…' he said, 'let's wait a bit. So it feels more… less…'

'We've probably got what, like seventy years or so? So yeah, we can wait a bit,' I said.

'Yeah. More like eighty years, if we factor in the advances in medicine that will happen over the course of our lives.'

'Well. That sounds like plenty of time to me.'

'Me too,' Sam smiled.

Oh no – I want to kiss him, I drunkenly thought. *What the hell is wrong with me?!* I took an awkward step back. 'Shall we go find the others?' I suggested.

We descended once more into the sweaty jungle. Sam led me to the VIP area behind the DJ booth. M and Julie were sitting at a table with some old official-looking guys, one of whom I assumed was Julie's uncle. There was a bottle of champagne in an ice bucket on the table, and M was serving herself liberally. She filled up another flute when she spotted me. I drank it quickly, feeling very aware of Sam next to me. The bubbles seemed to explode directly into my head.

Things blend in a little after that. Endless champagne bottles appeared. We danced lots more, going between the dancefloor and the VIP area depending on the vibe we were feeling. Sam and Julie left. I may have hugged Julie. M got to speak to her hero when the club closed, after which she was hyper and decided to join some friends at a house party. I got an uber to Dad's.

Cut to today.

Monday 24th October – evening

After writing, I went about my day doing things completely unrelated to maths, school, solving mysteries, or anything useful in any way. I have to say, it was a very pleasant way to spend time. For example, I:

– did two *Yoga with Adriene* classes, though with rather more child's pose than suggested.

– finished *Wild Wild Country* on Netflix and then fell into a Wikipedia hole about cults.

– read at least ten of the *Guardian* blind dates. Best line: *I imagine she thought of me what I think about people who live in Clapham.*

– made requests on six items on Depop.

– read pages 230-276 of *Dune* so I can give Oli his book back one day. (Fine, I'm really into it. I might even use FremenC as a username one day.)

It was sunny and bright outside, one of those days that you can convince yourself is summer as long as you don't go out to actually test the temperature – not that I felt any wish or any physical ability to go out.

I had my window open and someone nearby was playing Edward Sharpe and the Magnetic Zeros, which is Sam's favourite band. I cringed a bit at the recollection of last night – why had I been so awkward bumping into him? All the things I'd wished to say to him the past week, and when I got the chance, nothing came out. But I really think we'll be friends one day. In a few months... or years... Hopefully by then I'll be able to be drunk in his vicinity without being an idiot. Or we can have an alcohol-free friendship! That still counts, right?

Emma and Mum were giggling together in Emma's room so I went to see what they were up to. Mum asked if I was going to see Ty soon, without a) bringing up Sam or b) suggesting I invite Ty over so she can meet him and learn every single little detail of his life immediately. I obviously said not one word about where I'd recently spent the night, just told her we had a very proper and chaste cinema date planned for tonight.

I sat down on Emma's bed, watching the two of them as they went through Emma's wardrobe to get rid of too-small clothes. Oh dear, I've not been paying enough attention to her sense of style – I'll have to make sure to go along next time she goes shopping for new stuff. We all giggled as Emma tried on pyjamas that made her look like Alice in Wonderland after the *drink-me* potion. *Am I crazy*, I thought, *or... is everything going well at once?*

Obviously, that's when my phone rang. I walked out before answering. It was Ty.

Me: Hello?

Ty: Clara! Can you come over now? Before the cinema? Oli's here. He got away from our parents. He wants to talk to us, and he refuses to say a word until you come. So...

Me: Ok. [I laughed at his impatient tone] I'll come now.

Ty: And what about M. Are you with her?

Me: I'm not. But I'll tell her to come.

I smiled to myself and hung up. Oh well — I knew it couldn't last. I suppose twenty-four hours of normal life was a pretty good run. And I certainly made the most of it.

I texted M, who obviously answered right away that she was in. I changed quickly into black bootcut trousers and a mesh tiger-print top. I added my chain belt. Perfect. There was no point looking as bad as last time, was there?

I poked my head back into Emma's room, where they had moved on to sifting through a mountain of pink T-shirts, and said goodbye. I felt excited as I waited for the bus to Ty's. Fine — maybe normal life wasn't what I wanted after all.

Oli and Ty came out when I arrived and we went to a café round the corner. Oli got us both coffees and a tea for himself. M joined us a few minutes later and got an orange juice. She was wearing a gold cord jacket and her brown cord pants. Her undereye circles were as bad as mine but her attitude was a lot more chipper. I usually avoid her after going out, she's annoyingly impervious.

'So?' Ty asked once everyone was settled, staring at his brother. I could tell he'd been pretty impatient having to wait for us to arrive.

'First of all,' Oli said, 'I want some ground rules. I am going to tell you the full story because I can see that not giving you all the details last time was the wrong decision, but—'

'—no shit,' Ty rolled his eyes.

'Right. The first rule is no more interruptions from you.' Oli pinched Ty's shoulder playfully. 'The second rule is you guys can help, but not if you are putting yourselves in any danger.'

'Yes, yes,' Ty said.

M and I nodded dutifully.

'I mean it!' Oli pressed. 'If you plan to walk straight into a SPAM HQ again then—'

'—then you'll stay locked up to teach us a lesson?' M suggested.

'You'll make us solve computing problems this time,' I said.

'You'll wait for Karim's *unsophisticated efforts* to find you,' Ty said.

Oli sighed and smiled. 'Great, I can tell it's going to be really easy working with you all.'

'So we've agreed the rules,' Ty said. 'Now will you tell us?'

'We don't seem to have agreed any rules at all, but never mind.' Oli took a sip of his tea, then he put his cup down. We all looked at him expectantly. 'I want to stop SPAM for good,' he said lightly. 'And, you know, maybe your help could come in useful.'

Stop SPAM! Us?! I exchanged excited glances with M. Then we all started talking at once.

Me: What's your plan?

M: Why can't GCHQ do it?

Ty: Why did SPAM lock you up?

Oli took another sip of his tea. He was obviously enjoying this part.

'Well, I guess the first thing you should know is that I was working with GCHQ.' He raised his eyebrows.

M: You were *what*?!

Me: You mean all this was on purpose?

Ty: And you don't think you could have told me this in advance?

'Do you guys literally never stop asking questions?' Oli complained. 'If you would just stop interrupting, I could tell you the whole story from the beginning: when GCHQ approached me with a plan to catch Spencer.' Oli looked around at us and we were obediently silent, so he went on. 'They knew that my profile was exactly what Spencer was after right now – they'd been tracking his activities, and they knew he was low on money. He's been attempting more high-profile political stunts recently and his last money-making scheme was a while ago. Someone with my background would be pretty irresistible for him. So they got me on Spencer's radar – I posted on the HKZN forum, I briefly hacked into his phone… The aim was to do just enough to get him interested in me and suggest a meeting himself, so he'd think the idea had come from him. Until that point, everything went perfectly to plan. I was supposed to meet Spencer, leave and report back, and that would be the extent of my involvement. But instead, when I went to the meeting, there was no Spencer – just four hired guys who grabbed me as soon as I walked in, drove me away and put me in the locked room. You know what happened after that.'

M squinted at him. 'How... How could it go that wrong? That sounds like a total disaster!'

'Indeed,' Oli said simply. 'I mean, GCHQ are meant to be among the more competent of our prized national organisations, so this was a real mess-up. Unless... Spencer *knew* I was with GCHQ. All this time I believed he was falling into our trap, when actually *I* was falling right into *his*.'

We all stared at him, and then started speaking at once.

Ty: You think someone at GCHQ is leaking him information?

Me: Or Spencer has hacked GCHQ?

M: Or one of the cleaners is smuggling info out of the trash? What? [she raised her hands] Is that too vintage?

Oli laughed. 'Whichever one it is, we're going to find out.' He frowned. 'I started suspecting something just before I went for the meeting, actually. SPAM only ever contacted me when I was nowhere near the GCHQ building. It could have been coincidence, of course, but the timing was always so perfect. I thought I was being paranoid, but I still decided to leave you a one-time pad, Ty. Just in case.' he looked around at us. 'We're going to figure out exactly how the two of them are linked, and then we're going to get both of them.' He winked. 'So… are you in?'

We all nodded, some of us more enthusiastically than others.

'If we could also get the money back, that might help out my mum's husband,' I suggested. 'On the other hand, if he gets fired, he'll spend more time at home which she might be happy about. So, no pressure.'

'Or!' M said, 'we could get the money and, you know, give it to *someone else*.' She wiggled her eyebrows.

Oli laughed. 'No personal gain. That's the rule.'

'But if *you're* giving *me* the money, that's not *personal* gain,' M joked.

'How do we start?' Ty butted in, interrupting M mid-eyelash-batting.

Oli stretched his arms high up to the ceiling. 'I haven't thought through the details,' he said. 'I'm still down a few nights of sleep. Did I mention there was no mattress in that basement room? But those photos you took when you got me out, Ty – those are Spencer's notes on his next big project.' He dropped his arms back to his sides. 'That seems like a good starting point, don't you think?'

Suddenly my phone buzzed, interrupting our thoughts. I took it out.

'Oh my god,' I whispered, 'I got it right?'

'What? What is it?' Ty asked.

I turned my phone round so they could all see. I'd got an email from an unknown sender. The subject said *An Invitation*, and when I opened it, there was just one line with a signature:

Congratulations. We invite you to follow the link below to access the next stage.

HKZN

THE END

ACKNOWLEDGMENTS

Thank you first of all to both of my parents for passing on, each in their own way, their love of maths (my mum by doing all my homework with me because 'it's so much fun!' and my dad by setting me maths problems and then refusing to ever give me the answers even if it took me years solve them).

Thanks, again, to my mum, for being my first reader, my last reader and many readers in between, and for finding me funny. Sorry I took out some of your favourite bits.

Thank you to my other readers, Natacha, Cécile, Abby (also the perfect Clara voice on the audio book), Alex, Mimi - you all read very different versions, from the first one over ten years ago to the one that's out in the world now. It was so fun for me to see you get sucked in to the story and laugh at Clara's adventures - and it was also the best motivation to get the book actually finished.

Thank you to everyone who said this book sounded like a great idea when I told them about it, I hope you were right! Thank you for all the extra stuff that goes into a book, for words of encouragement, anecdotes, teaching me about the English school system and discussing whether Ty would be a skater (thanks Rowan), listening to me when I thought I was about to become a super famous author and encouraging me to self-publish when that didn't happen.

Thanks finally (though slightly grumpily) to the publishing professionals who saw the manuscript. Even though it didn't work out in the end, I was lucky enough to get great edit notes from agents and editors at some big-name publishing houses, and all of them helped to make the book so much better.

Coralie Colmez is the daughter of two mathematicians. She studied maths at Cambridge university and wrote a popular maths book called *Math on Trial* with her mother. For her day job, Coralie runs the education platform Unifrog with her husband - maybe you spotted the shout-out in the book!

Lightning Source UK Ltd.
Milton Keynes UK
UKHW020701251022
411061UK00016B/1267